Follow the author on Twitter: @edmontonnoir
Follow the author on Instagram: @edmontonnoir
Email the author: edmontonnoir@protonmail.com

MIDNIGHT DRIVE

First edition. June 1, 2022.

Written by Kenneth Price.

For my mother Anne and my wife Julie.

Midnight Drive

1

The front doors of the Klondike Casino were covered with plywood because someone drove their truck through them the week before.

A piece of computer paper stuck to the plywood advised patrons to enter through the fire exit on the south side of the building until the doors could be repaired, and apologised for the inconvenience.

Inside, VLTs chimed and rang. Their purple neon light pushed back against the harsh white fluorescence from the kitchen behind the bar. There, hunkered over the bar, a group of young thugs in baggy t-shirts and ball caps watched football replays overhead and slipped their own booze into pints of Coke long after last call.

It was the zero-hour. A place in no-time in the middle of the night when Logan felt at peace. The casino walls kept the outside world outside and, inside, the numbers ruled the room. If Logan could perceive them well enough he might catch a numbers wave and ride it as long as it would carry him.

Even if a thousand trucks hurtled at the exterior of the Klondike Casino, the interior would still remain as immovable and timeless as ever. The zero-hour felt as though even if the Earth exploded, the Klondike Casino would continue to exist in its own kind of heaven. The people perched at the VLTs would always be there. The Top 40 hits would play on. The boys at the bar would forever be slipping cheap rye into their pints of Coke. In heaven, faces come and go at the poker table and Logan would watch the numbers play out in their great cosmic order.

The big blind orbited the table, the small blind followed in its wake, and Logan folded on anything that wasn't a couple of face cards. Or at least suited Jack-Tens. The speakers in the ceiling pumped in a steady pulse of Shania Twain and Justin Timberlake. Pit bosses did their rounds, marching around the floor right on time like characters on a cuckoo clock. The hot dogs rolling on the warmer at the end of the bar, too, gave the impression they had been rotating there for an eternity. Their leathery smell seeped over to the table where Logan pressed the two cards down with the palm of his hand and lifted the corners.

A pair of kings. An eighty-two percent chance of winning against any two other cards. Fifty-fifty against four other players pre-flop.

The dealer was an older lady with frizzy grey hair. A professional smile was etched in her face that otherwise drooped downward. She looked through the players' chests at something beyond them as she slung cards to each player at a steady rhythm.

A Russian in a black shirt and gold chain sat to Logan's left and made ludicrous bets here and there, sometimes going in on an unsuited Ten-Six or a Jack-Two when there was clearly nothing to be gained.

Next to him, a drunk farmer in a thick plaid jacket and rumpled mesh-back John Deere cap nodded off and occasionally needed an elbow from the Russian when it was his turn to bet. The dealer tut-tutted it might be time to pack it in but the farmer insisted he was fine to stay.

On the far end of the table two Somali cab drivers had finished the late-night bar rush and came to the poker table to clean out whatever drunks came in feeling lucky.

One of the cabbies occasionally gave his cards a sharp thwack against the table, as though to straighten them. The other responded by picking up a stack of chips between his fingers and letting them scuttle to the table.

Logan bet half the pot — enough to stoke interest without scaring anyone away. The farmer and one of the cabbies folded. Logan felt his canine tooth with his tongue as he calculated the odds of winning now two players had dropped out. Somewhere around sixty-eight percent.

The flop came down — a two, a nine, and a queen.

The other cabbie folded leaving only Logan and the Russian. Eighty-two percent chance of winning. Logan pushed a stack of chips toward the centre of the table.

"You bet like big boy," said the Russian. His sleepy eyes looked out from dark, heavy eyelids. "Is good."

The Russian limped in with a fifty dollar raise and Logan raised again with another hundred dollars.

Through the turn — a three, and the river — an eight, Logan leaned forward and made no other expressive gestures. With all five cards facing up and Logan with an eighty-seven percent chance of winning, he and the Russian parried back and forth with their bets. The Russian pushed back. Logan slid the rest of his chips to the centre of the table.

Something in the air seemed to pop.

Logan turned his cards over and didn't even need to see the Russian's hand. The gravity in the room got heavier. Logan's shoulders buckled under some invisible weight and his guts sank down into his colon.

"You bet like man with maybe pair of kings," said the Russian, and nodded in agreement of his own assessment.

The room spun in a blur of lights. All the guts that sank into his lower intestine turned into red hot bile and rose up into his chest.

The Russian turned over a two of hearts and a two of clubs to complement the two of diamonds on the table. Three of a kind.

The surging bile in Logan's chest rose up into his throat and exploded out of his face in a pure hot stream of invectives.

As the Russian pulled in the chips toward himself, Logan threw his cards into his face.

"Fuck you, you fucking piece of shit," yelled Logan. "You bet like a bitch commie, you fucking Stalinist coward asshole."

The Russian stared back at him, expressionless as a dead whale.

"You fucking hear me, asshole?" Logan continued. He turned to the dealer who was waving over other staff. "You just going to stand there and let this asshole desecrate your game like that? It's fucking vandalism against the integrity of the game."

The taxi drivers picked up their chips and backed away from the table as a woman in a pantsuit strode across the floor with security in tow.

"Sir, SIR," she started.

"'Sir sir' yeah yeah yeah," said Logan. "This fucking Russian is betting like a fucking Russian."

"We're going to ask you to leave now, Mr. Claybourne," said the woman. Each of the security guards grabbed an elbow and walked Logan staggering backwards to the exit.

Logan's body surged forward against the drag of the security guards pulling him backward.

"And how can you not see those cabbies are colluding? Do your fucking jobs! This casino is amateur hour."

The casino patrons pretended not to notice as the security guards mustered into a small group and corralled Logan toward the fire exit. Gus, the head of security, waited at the coat check holding Logan's backpack. They dropped Logan down at his feet.

Gus looked down at Logan with one side of his mouth up-ticked into a little smirk. From the floor, Logan looked up at the underside of Gus' belly, slightly exposed beneath the black Klondike Casino shirt that was one size too small. Logan stood up and went to grab his backpack. Gus didn't let go.

"Come on, man," said Logan.

Logan pulled at his backpack again and Gus held his grip on it.

"Hey, Gus, I'm sorry. I lost a lot of money back there and I got a little excited. It's stupid. I apologize."

A dumb smile widened on Gus' face. Logan yanked the backpack toward him and Gus yanked it back.

"Give me my stuff, you fat fuck!" Logan shouted as he pushed Gus backward. The backpack fell out of Gus' hands as he fell into the dark coat check counter.

The people who pretended not to notice the commotion before now stopped and stared. Logan picked up his backpack and turned toward the exit. He made it a couple steps when a large hand twisted his right arm behind his back and another grabbed him by the neck. Gus used Logan's face to open the door.

Outside Gus clocked him in the head a couple of times, which wasn't as bad as the slug to the stomach. It knocked the wind out of Logan and he crumpled to the sidewalk gasping for air. Gus dropped the backpack onto his head.

"You're barred for two weeks, Logan," said Gus.

Logan tried to tell him where to shove those two weeks but Gus turned back toward the door before he could suck in enough air to speak.

Logan stretched out flat on his back on the sidewalk and bent at the knees until he worked up enough air in his lungs to stand up. He staggered to his feet and leaned back against the brick wall of the casino, still gasping short, sharp breaths.

Once he pulled himself together, he lumped his way toward the parking lot.

A black BMW pulled up to the curb. A large, bald man got out of the driver's seat and left the car running. Tom. Tom had a scar over his eyebrow and wore small hoop earrings.

"Man, not tonight," Logan protested.

Tom slugged Logan in the gut, sending Logan crumpling to the pavement again. He rolled onto his hands and knees, choking in gasps of hot air. Tom walked back to the car and opened the back door.

"Let's go," said Tom.

Logan didn't move so Tom grabbed Logan by the back of his shirt and pulled him up.

"Go fuck yourself," Logan croaked.

Tom shoved Logan in the back of the car like a pile of luggage. By the time Logan sat upright they were speeding down the Fort Road turnoff onto the Yellowhead Highway.

2

Logan stretched out in the back seat. Tom floored it, pushing the black BMW into all it could handle rounding the curves. Logan watched the headlights of the traffic roll across the headliner and the first blue hints of sunrise began to gush behind them.

"You didn't have to hit me, Tom," said Logan.

"I'm not a taxi driver," said Tom. "If I didn't hit you, I wouldn't be doing my job. It's for making me come and get you."

Logan nodded a sardonic smile and worked to take long, slow breaths.

"Aw, come on," said Tom. "I'm sorry. Want a sucker?"

Tom held out a bag of lollipops without taking his eyes off the road. Logan glared at him through the rear-view mirror before giving in and taking a red sucker out of the bag and popping it in his mouth.

"Why does he want to see me in the middle of the night?"

"It's six o'clock in the morning," said Tom.

"Why does Ricky want to see me at six o'clock then?"

"Cuz that's when we know where to find you."

Logan closed his eyes and felt the car's movements through a series of stops and starts and turns as they swung off the Yellowhead and down 97th Street and jerked its way down 118th Avenue. When it came to rest, the various neon colours of the Champion City Pawn signs washed over Logan's face.

Tom shut off the car and walked around to the other side toward the pawn shop entrance. Iron cages covered the windows. Posters behind the glass read 'Cash for Gold' and 'Payday Loans.' The OPEN sign was off but the orange CHAMPION CITY PAWN sign buzzed brightly next to the larger red neon sign that simply read PAWN in capital letters, and a blue neon sign reading LOANS. Their colours reflected in the wet street.

Tom turned back and nodded for Logan to get out of the car. Logan climbed out and Tom locked the car with a chirp from his keys. He unlocked the front door of the shop and locked it behind them once they were inside.

It was dark but a green glow from the back room allowed them to navigate their way past the tables of old tools and lawn mowers and televisions.

They made their way through the backroom of shelves packed to the ceiling with people's collateral - stereos, snowboards, guitars. The door of the large bank safe was closed — the shop took the space over from a defunct bank that shut down years before Champion City Pawn moved in.

Logan followed Tom downstairs and they squeezed their way down a hall lined with bicycles.

Tom pulled a string tied to a chain to illuminate the single bulb hanging from the office ceiling.

A couple of ripped and faded office chairs faced a simple desk in a room of cinder block walls painted green.

Logan finished his sucker and tossed the stick into the dented metal trashcan by the desk. Tom and Logan sat next to each other as they listened to Logan's brother-in-law Ricky urinate in the washroom across the hall from the office. It was a strong piss, a steady torrent that didn't taper off. It ended abruptly with the toilet bowl still resonating from the barrage. They listened to the toilet flush and Ricky zip up.

Ricky was gay but had also married Logan's sister Clare regardless. It was none of Logan's business so he didn't ask any questions. Ricky certainly cared for Clare. They enjoyed their time together and Ricky gave her a comfortable life. It also seemed he was able to put all his property in her name so he could skirt around various laws. If the feds ever came knocking he could pull the chute and not much could touch him. Clare wanted a companion but nothing sexual. Ricky saw his boyfriends on his own time. So it was a match made in heaven.

Logan was also sure Ricky enjoyed a sort of collateral influence over him as well, now that they were family and all.

Cowboy boots stomped across the hall and Ricky exploded through the door like a disco locomotive. He wore a sequined country-western shirt, silver in colour, tucked into jeans so tight his package bulged at the front. His hair was slicked back and an aggressive mustache bristled straight out from his face. A cigarette stuck out from between his teeth and clouds of smoke chuffed out of his face around it.

"Logan, buddy, what's going on?" he asked.

"You don't need to send Tom to get me," said Logan.

"I was worried about you," he said, his attention on squaring off some stacks of papers on his desk. "Your rent paid up?"

"It's fine," said Logan.

"Oh good. It's fine. For a second I was worried you took my money and pissed it away at the casino."

"I can get your money," said Logan. "It's not a big deal."

Ricky arched his back backwards until it cracked.

"You see, Logan, it is a big deal. It's kind of a big fucking deal. When you take someone's money, they tend to get upset. I'm upset. I'm downright cranky about it. I loaned you that money to help you. So you could pay your rent, and then I find out you've thrown it all away at the 'Dike. For normal people, that's enough to be friends-off. Maybe they block you on social media and they're done with you for life. But I'm your brother-in-law. And I'm a business man. When people run off with my money —"

"I didn't run off with it," said Logan. "I can pay you back."

"When people run off with my money," Ricky repeated, "I react in firm but fair ways to prevent these mistakes from happening again. Tom, what happened to Thunder Bay Ray?"

Tom stood behind Logan and cracked his knuckles.

"Broke his nose," said Tom.

"Kicked him around the alley and broke his goddamn nose," said Ricky. "Thunder Bay pawned a kid's ATV in my shop. Turns out it was, A, stolen. Of course. And, B, wouldn't even start. Very next day I have the pawn cop crawling up my ass accusing me of theft and breaking some kid's heart over some junk that doesn't even work. Of course, Thunder Bay had no intention of coming back for it. Now Thunder Bay Ray whistles when he blows his nose."

"So you going to kick my ass now or what?" said Logan.

"Logan," Ricky cooed like he was talking to a cocker spaniel. "You're my brother-in-law. You're family. I don't want to rough you up. I mean, I will if I have to. But I don't want to. It's going to make my life that much more difficult if you start coming over to Thanksgiving dinner with black eyes. That day's coming, I'm sure, but I'm not ready for that yet and neither are you."

Ricky stood in front of Logan and Logan turned his head away from the bulge in Ricky's pants.

Ricky picked up the trash can and stabbed out his cigarette in the dent and dropped the butt in. He sat back on the corner of the the desk, scraping crud out of the corner of his eye with his pinky finger.

"Clare wants to go to school," said Ricky.

"That's good," said Logan.

"She's come a long way," said Ricky. "She wants to take Interior Design, which suits me just fine. God, I've been wanting to do something with the lighting in our place forever. Something more modern. But the point is, Logan, I can't afford to take care of the both of you."

Logan glared at Ricky.

"If you have the money, give it back and that can go toward Clare's textbooks," said Ricky.

Logan's face darkened and he shook his head slightly.

"That's what I thought," said Ricky. "Tell you what. There's something you can do."

Ricky opened the file drawer in the desk and ducked down as he rifled through the papers. He reappeared with several papers in his hand.

"A Corvette," he said, tossing the papers on top of the desk. "Plus, an additional loan to fix it up."

Logan flipped through the papers. Ricky gave a loan to a guy named Kenny Prince for the purchase of a 1976 Corvette Stingray. Plus, an additional loan to put in a new compressor, condenser, bushings, ball joints, custom hybrid fuel injection, and a paint job in metallic amethyst blue.

"And I guess he defaulted?" asked Logan.

"Got himself fucking killed is what he did," said Ricky. "Two nights ago. Cops are crawling all over the place right now. I need you to get the car before the cops decide they want to impound it. Says there in black and white I'm the lawful owner of that car and possession is nine tenths of the law. If that car ends up in a police impound lot it'll take me a year at least to get that car out and cost me even more money. But if I've got it, then they need a warrant to seize it. So they'd need a pretty good reason."

A photocopy of Kenny's driver's license hung diagonally at the bottom of the last page. A splotchy driver's licence photo showed a man with dark, wild eyes and a handlebar moustache.

"That's a photocopy of the contract so you can hang on to that," said Ricky. "Kenny was only a couple payments from owning it outright. Damn shame. His address is on his license at the bottom. I drove by there yesterday and didn't see the Stingray. Did you ever know Kenny?"

"No."

The memory made Ricky smile.

"Kenny, ah, Kenny enjoyed the finer things in life. Crack cocaine, booze, and strippers mostly. He looked like an older Hulk Hogan in a cowboy hat. He was high as elephant balls when he came in here with a couple chickies on his arm and announced he wanted that Stingray."

Ricky's eyes glazed over with memories. Logan and Tom waited for whatever they were to percolate to the top.

"There was one time," Ricky said, still watching the memory play at the front of his mind. "You see, he operated sump trucks for a living. He was caught dumping God-knows-what into a city sewer. It was a female arresting officer and he slapped her on the ass and said, 'You'll never catch me alive!' and tried to hop back in his truck. But she caught him. Oh, she caught him alright. He spent the night in jail. Charged with assaulting a police officer but the charge was dropped later."

He trailed off as the details of the memory slipped away from him.

"He was a good guy though. I haven't gotten to the best part. Go find the 'Vette, bring it back and I'll mark our loan agreement as paid in full. I'll tear our contract right up. We're even. Easy peasy. Alright?"

Logan took a deep breath and nodded.

"Once that car is back, I can flip it and that car will pay for Clare's tuition by itself," said Ricky. "She'd like that. I'd appreciate it. You'd really be helping her out. There's a couple more here too."

He picked up some more papers and tapped their ends against the table to square them and placed them back down again.

"But start with the Corvette," said Ricky. "See how you do with that, and then come back for these other ones and there'll be a bit more money in it for you.

Logan lifted his gaze from the contracts back to Ricky. Logan folded the Stingray agreement and put it in his pocket.

"Cool?" said Ricky.

Logan felt his pockets. For what, he wasn't sure. Tom motioned toward the door like he was bored of the conversation and ready to move on with his day.

"If there's no keys, call me and I'll send Tom over with the tow truck," said Ricky, looking at his watch. Then he looked up at Logan. "You got a phone?"

Logan shook his head no.

"Pawned it? Pawned it with someone else? Why, I'm offended," said Ricky, holding one hand over his heart and gasping in mock insult. His lips slid into a wide open smile, revealing a few gold teeth. "Tom, grab Logan a phone upstairs, eh?"

Logan followed Tom upstairs as Ricky sat back behind the desk. He lit another cigarette and started texting someone furiously and grumbled to himself about whoever he was texting.

Upstairs, Tom unlocked a cabinet next to the large safe and pulled out a plastic basket full of cell phones, each one in a plastic sandwich bag with a pawn ticket. Tom flipped through them until he found a suitable one.

"Pissy Chrissie pawned this one," he said, handing one to Logan. "No way she's coming back for it. The password's on the back of the ticket."

3

The odds of being murdered in this country are 1.8:1000 — about the same as drawing a straight flush in Texas Hold 'Em. However, you are dealt many hands in poker. But you only get one life. Eventually your number comes up.

Then again, some might say with every decision we make we are dealt a new hand. It stands to reason every time you make a decision - where to go to school, who you befriend, which way you walk to the grocery store - you change course in life. A new spectrum of probable ends unfold. And yet again, in the end, maybe no matter what decisions we make perhaps that 1.8:1000 remains about the same as it did in the first place anyway. Maybe fate is just the odds playing out.

Kenny Prince played his hand. Yellow police tape wrapped around a bare, skinny tree and stretched across the front yard to the last post on a dilapidated wooden fence that ran into the back yard. The face of the little bungalow sunk into the Earth and the front steps bowed in the middle, their paint almost completely scuffed away and revealing grey, splintered wood underneath. A crack streaked across the glass in the screen door and the top corner of the flyscreen was ripped out from the frame and hung limply in the air. No Corvettes presented themselves out front so Logan walked around the block to the back alley.

The property sat on 86th Street, a couple blocks north of Commonwealth Stadium, between two tall condominium towers — one to the south with several colourful panels like a Mondrian painting, and the other to the north shimmering with reflective blue glass. A muddy, unpaved parking space in a patch of grass faced the alley. Logan looked up at the balconies of each condo tower before lifting the latch on the back gate and letting himself into the backyard. The gate door hung crookedly and its bottom corner dug into the ground. Logan leaned into it with his shoulder to open it.

The backyard was large enough to play soccer in if the grass wasn't overgrown. A couple beer cans littered the backyard along with a grungy pair of black panties and a ladder left haphazardly in the long grass. A hot tub situated itself a few steps from the back door — off-kilter from the side of the house, as though it were dropped from the sky and hooked up as it landed without any rearrangement of its position whatsoever. A mostly finished bottle of cheap champagne perched on the edge of the tub. On the ground, loose and broken paving stones surrounded the hot tub unevenly.

The back door was locked. Logan looked up at each of the condo towers again and then climbed up the hot tub ladder onto the edge of the hot tub. From there, he slid open the kitchen window. With a jump he was able to hook his arm around the inside wall and hoist himself through the window and tumbled over the sink onto the floor.

The inside of the house smelled of stale beer and years of smoking. Dishes filled the sink. A wall calendar lay on the floor. Empty cans and bottles covered the round dining table and all the counter spaces, which Logan scanned carefully for car keys.

The house still held the energy of violent movement you could trace like brush strokes around the room. Chairs were upended. Photographs and chinaware spilled out of a cabinet onto the floor.

He opened all the kitchen drawers. He opened the fridge only to find a bowl of congealed macaroni with a dollop of ketchup encrusted on the side.

The master bedroom contained a large unkempt bed and a television against the wall opposite it. The dresser was empty. Clothes covered the floor. Logan picked up every pair of jeans and felt the pockets. He kicked around the t-shirts and underwear on the floor, listening for the jangle of keys but there was none. A plastic baggie of marijuana lay on the nightstand with an ashtray filled with the stubbed ends of joints.

Logan walked back down the hall to the living room.

A spray of blood splashed against the wall over the couch. More blood hardened into a crusty brown paste soaked into the couch. The coffee table was thrown on its side against the wall under another television. Empty beer cans and dirty dishes scattered across the floor.

Logan looked closer and above the couch a square QR code was slapped against the wall amongst the splatter of darkening blood.

Logan shook his head and walked out of the room, back along the hall and down the stairs next to the washroom to the basement.

Downstairs, a worn old sofa faced a small television in an unfinished basement surrounded by bare concrete walls. Blankets lay strewn across the sofa. A glass crack pipe and a plastic bong sat on the coffee table in front it. A brown workout bench and barbell collected dust in the corner.

Logan lifted the couch cushions, found nothing underneath them, and went back upstairs. He took a deep breath before going back to the living room.

A violent energy still hung in the air. The shadows seemed to rear back into the cracks and corners as if there was a fire at the centre of the room. Logan hesitated before stepping into the room but then edged his way in. He lifted one end of the coffee table and poked around the end tables. Key hooks by the front door were bare. He returned to the couch - a sandy corduroy fabric soaked through with hardened blood. A police marker with the number one on it stood at the centre of the patch of blood on the couch.

He looked up at the QR code on the wall. It was a sticker. It lay over top a couple thin streaks of blood. He pulled the phone out of his pocket and scanned the QR code. The browser on his phone redirected a couple times before coming to a 404 page saying the destination could not be reached.

Logan pinched the corner of the couch cushion between his fingers and lifted. There were no keys but forty dollars in twenties lay stuck between the cushions, a line of blood striped across the fold in the centre. Logan pinched the money out and shoved it into his pocket.

He walked back out, giving the living room and kitchen a careful last glance. He let himself out the back door and followed the path to the front sidewalk.

The clouds had parted since Logan went inside the house. Logan put his head down and made quick strides as he made his way down the road but didn't get far before a burgundy SUV pulled out from where it was parked along the curb and crept along behind him. It chirped out a police car's 'whoop whoop' and then red and blue flashers blinked on.

The passenger side window rolled down as the car pulled up next to Logan.

"Come here," said the driver.

Logan's right leg took a half a step to run but Logan corrected himself and sidled up to the passenger window. The police officer inside wore plain clothes, a hoodie and a flat brim ball cap. He had a thick neck and he stared penetratingly at Logan's face.

"What's your name?" he asked.

"Logan. Logan Claybourne."

"You have some ID?"

Logan fished his driver's license out of his wallet and handed it over. The officer examined it and typed onto his laptop.

"You want to tell me what you were doing in a crime scene, Logan?" he asked.

"I'm a repo man. I was sent to find a car."

"Who do you work for?"

"Four Five Five Seventeen Ninety Holdings Limited," said Logan.

"Woah woah, say that again," said the officer.

Logan repeated Ricky's company name and the officer typed it into his computer.

"I'm going to have to ask you to get in. Need to ask you some questions."

"Am I under arrest?"

"I haven't decided yet," said the officer.

Logan opened the back door and got in.

4

A couple cops worked the front desk behind thick glass windows at police headquarters. A woman towing along five kids complained to the cop in the first window about something to do with her noisy neighbours and the cop listened patiently. His face sagged as he couldn't be bothered to muster much real concern. At the second window, a homeless man accused the other officer of covering up the existence of space aliens. Both cops stared far beyond the complainants in front of them as though they questioned their own life decisions.

The plain-clothed officer escorted Logan from the front door with a tight grip on Logan's elbow. The two cops looked up at them with vague interest in their bored faces before returning to the people nattering at them through the windows.

He lifted a counter and they passed through a door, around a corner, and down a hall lined with offices on either side. It led to a quiet area deep within a maze of hallways. He opened the door to an interview room with a table, three chairs and camera high up in the upper corner of the room.

"Have a seat," said the officer. "I'll be right back. Can I get you anything?"

"No thanks," said Logan.

The officer left the room and Logan studied the picked-away laminate on the edge of the table in front of him and counted the holes in the ceiling tiles.

When the officer eventually returned he had another officer with him. The other guy was white, older, bushy cop mustache and wore a golf shirt with a badge hanging in front of him.

The first officer held a cup of coffee in a Styrofoam cup and placed it down in front of Logan.

"Got you a coffee anyway," he said. "My name is Detective Darius Days. My colleague here is Detective Harrison. You're not under arrest. We just want to ask you a few questions, OK?"

Detective Days was relaxed, his voice steady and rhythmic.

"What's your name?"

"Logan Claybourne."

"What were you doing at our crime scene today, Logan?"

"I'm a repo man. My boss sent me to get his car."

Days asked the questions. Harrison sat back with his arms folded and studied Logan's responses.

"Who is your employer?"

"Four Five Five One Seven Nine Zero Holdings Limited," said Logan.

Detective Days' face soured.

"Your boss' name. What's your boss' name?"

"Ricky Nunez."

"You got a number for Ricky?"

"Four One Four - Seven Three Four Two."

"Mind if we call him?"

"Go for it."

Inspector Harrison pulled a phone out of his pocket and left the room.

"You been working a long time for Ricky Nunez?" asked Days.

"Off and on," said Logan.

"How do you like being a repo man?" asked Days. "Gotta be times it gets interesting."

"It's a dream come true," said Logan.

Days closed his eyes and nodded. Then he opened his eyes to look at Logan's face and Logan looked right back.

The room was cold in a way that didn't seem to affect Detective Days. Logan leaned forward with his elbows on his thighs and lowered his chin into his chest.

After a couple minutes Harrison came back into the room and gave a nod to Days.

"Were you aware you were walking into an active crime scene investigation today?" Days continued.

"No."

"You didn't see the yellow police tape everywhere?"

"I guess I wasn't paying attention."

"Did you find anything?"

Logan shook his head.

"What did you see?"

"Nothing."

"Nothing?" said Days. "You didn't see blood all over the living room wall?"

"Yeah, I saw that."

"Do you know whose blood it was?"

"Not really," said Logan.

"Not really?" said Days. "Like you only somewhat know whose blood it is? What do you mean?"

"My boss said his customer Kenny Prince died and sent me to get the car. So, probably his blood I guess. Could not be too."

"Did you know Kenny Prince?"

"Nope," said Logan.

"What kind of car are you looking for?"

"1976 Chevrolet Corvette Stingray. Blue."

"A blue Stingray. That's more your speed, isn't it?" Days said to Harrison, giving him a little slap on the knee with the back of his hand. "Got kind of a Guns n' Roses vibe. You seem like a Guns n' Roses guy, eh Bob?"

Inspector Harrison gave no response. His attention stayed on Logan.

"I'm more into luxury cars, myself. BMW. Jaguars."

"What about you? You like Stingrays?"

Logan shrugged.

"C'mon man, you got to have some kind of opinion on a 1976 Corvette Stingray. Who doesn't have an opinion on a Stingray?"

"They're okay," Logan said, a reluctant tone in his voice. "The gears usually grind because of weak synchros."

Inspector Days slapped the table as he laughed.

"Well there you have it, Bob," he said. "Weak synchros on the Corvette Stingray. You find that a lot, do you?"

"Wouldn't be so bad if people didn't slam the gears when they shift," said Logan. "But it's a Stingray so that's exactly what everybody does to feel like a rock star."

"Sure," said Days, studying Logan's face and mulling something over in his mind. "I bet they do."

Detective Harrison stayed in the corner with his arms folded as his eyes scanned over Logan.

"Why don't you walk me backward from when I found you at the crime scene to where you were three nights ago?" said Days. "So before you were in Kenny Prince's house, where were you?"

"I woke up at home," said Logan.

"Where's that?"

"Apartment 304, 9513 118th Avenue," said Logan.

"And where were you before that?"

"I was in my boss' pawn shop, Champion City Pawn," said Logan. "He talked about repossessing the Corvette."

"OK, great," said Days. "Where were you before the pawn shop?"

"At the casino."

"Which casino?"

"Klondike."

"Great," said Days. "How'd you do at the casino?"

"Lost," said Logan.

"I'm sorry," said Day. "Where were you before that?"

"My apartment," said Logan.

"What did you do in your apartment?"

"Nothing."

"Nothing? You must have done something. You watch TV?"

"No," said Logan.

"You didn't do anything? Call a friend? Read a book?"

"No."

"You just sat at the kitchen table doing nothing?"

Logan lifted his hands with nothing to say.

"OK," said Days. "So the night before that, where were you?"

"Casino," said Logan.

"Casino again, OK. Same one?"

Logan shook his head.

"Millenium."

"Any better luck there?" asked Days.

"Broke even," said Logan.

Detective Harrison remained unmoved and studied Logan's responses.

"Day before that, what did you do?"

"Walked around. Pawned my phone. Walked around some more."

"And the night before that?"

"Hung out at home," said Logan.

"Doing nothing, I bet?" asked Days.

"Yeah," said Logan.

They repeated the conversation a couple more times before Detective Days decided he'd had enough and walked Logan out of the interview room, through the network of hallways and back to the front door of the station. As they walked, he advised Logan not to leave town and to let him know if he came across anything that might concern the investigation.

"If I find you rummaging around my crime scene, I'm going to arrest you. Understand?"

Logan said he understood. Days held the door open for Logan and flicked out a business card. "You let me know if you find that car, OK?"

Logan took the card and walked out across the street toward the bus stop.

"Hey, Logan," Days called after him. "Take it easy on those synchros."

5

Logan settled himself in a seat on the Eastwood bus behind the rear door, squeezing into the corner where the seat met the wall, and pulled the phone out of his pocket.

He searched for Kenny Prince on social media and it didn't take long before he found him. Kenny's social media footprint worked in mainly three genres: right-wing conspiracy theory memes and suggesting the government could kiss his ass, soft-core porn videos of strippers passing through town, and the third was photos of himself drinking in his hot tub, often accompanied by different young ladies half his age in bikinis.

Kenny was on the 'stopped giving a shit' side of middle age. In several photos he wore only a black leather swimsuit with his big gut hanging down over top of the waistband. A black cowboy hat complemented his blond and greying handlebar mustache that framed a fat cigar in almost every photograph.

He didn't mind showing off how good of a time he had. The photos were plentiful and exhibited little self-censorship.

In one photo he stood on the edge of his hot tub in only his little black swimsuit like a rock singer on stage and chugged a beer with the can extended half a foot from his face. Another photo showed a close-up of him retrieving a shot glass with his mouth from between a girl's breasts. Another showed him in the hot tub with two girls on his lap. The girls smiled but looked tired. Dark rings circled under their eyes and their cheeks bore a sallow complexion. Kenny, though, always had a twinkle in his eye.

Hundreds of accounts showed up as friends of Kenny Prince, although together they gave the sense Kenny was pretty indiscriminate about who he accepted friend requests from. It was difficult to tell which of those people Kenny knew in real life, or even how many of them were real people who existed in real life at all.

Logan scrolled and scrolled through images of a Las Vegas vacation until finally he came to Kenny Prince's birthday. July 4th. There was a message from a woman named Valerie Prince who called Kenny 'dad' and wished him a happy birthday. There was a brief exchange of pleasantries that ended with Valerie telling Kenny to take care of himself.

Logan clicked on her profile.

She wore nurse's scrubs. She didn't post very often. Most of her photos presented herself smiling politely with friends in various restaurants around town.

Logan sent a message to her.

"Hello, sorry to bother you," he wrote. "My name is Logan Claybourne. I'm a private detective assisting the police with the investigation. If I could briefly meet with you, I would appreciate it. It's kind of important."

He put the phone back in his pocket and leaned against the window as the bus rolled north on 95th Street.

Outside, homeless people lined up along the wall of a bottle depot with their shopping carts of empties. On the next block, men loitered along the fence of 'cash corner' looking for day labour jobs. Of course, that late in the day, the jobs had dried up and they spent their day sitting on their hard hats bumming cigarettes and passing the time.

Logan got off the bus on 118th Avenue. He stopped in at a samosa restaurant and picked up food with one of the twenty dollar bills he found in Kenny Prince's couch and carried the box of samosas back to his apartment building.

The building's front door opened to a musty smell of mildew and marijuana. He climbed the stairs to his apartment on the third floor.

Logan didn't have much furniture. A neighbour gave him the couch when they moved out, along with a cheap round dining table and a single dining chair. The brown vinyl upholstery of the other three chairs wore out until the foam poked through and they found their way to the dumpster. No television. He never watched it when he had one so he sold it a couple years ago to pay off a gambling debt.

He kept a map of the city tacked on the wall for when he needed to plan out a repossession while his phone was in pawn. Little pins stuck into it cast long shadows over the city when he turned on the kitchen light.

A bench press stood parallel to the patio window.

He toppled on to the couch and ate a samosa.

An overturned wooden packing crate served as a coffee table. From it, he picked up his deck of cards that rested next to a well-worn volume of The Expert at the Card Table by S. W. Erdnase, a classic treatise on card shuffling and deck manipulation.

Logan practiced card shuffling. The rhythmic movement worked the jitters out of his system and it was a kind of meditation. He sat with his hands folded in front of him, the cards riffling back and forth between them, his focus concentrated on the most subtle touches of his fingertips.

The phone in his pocket rang. It was his sister Clare.

"Hi, Logan."

She said she called to see how he was doing but with a clipped tone in her voice.

"Ricky said he got some work for you," she said.

"Yeah."

"That's good, right?"

"Yeah."

"You don't sound too happy about it. Why so glum, chum?"

"No, for sure," said Logan. "It's great. I'm happy."

A tense breath released out her nose and crackled out the phone speaker on Logan's end.

"He's doing you a favour, Logan," she said.

"I know."

They said nothing for a moment. Logan held the phone away from his head until she spoke again.

"He told me you gambled away the loan he gave you. What were you thinking?"

"He likes it. It means I'll work for him for free. We always do this."

"No, he doesn't like it, Logan. He's trying to help you but it seems like you don't want to help yourself."

A lump in her throat was choking up her words and she took another moment to breathe through it.

"I know what I'm doing, Clare. I would have five times that money he loaned me but there was a Russian at the table who cheated and the casino staff can't even do their jobs —"

"Other people always cheat, Logan," she interrupted. "You can't live your life like —"

The words stopped short in her throat again.

"This is the best it's ever been," she said. "Please don't ruin it."

The phone vibrated. Logan looked at it. It was a message from Valerie Prince.

"I got to go," said Logan.

"He's done nothing but try and help us, Logan."

"It's about the car. I got to go. Tell him thank you," said Logan and he hung up.

He looked at the message from Valerie.

It read, "I already spoke to the police."

Logan took a second to get into character.

"Hi Valerie," he wrote. "Thanks for getting in touch. We are still assessing the threat level. We think you are safe but there is some concern. I know this is a trying time for you but I'd like to ask you a few routine questions. It would greatly assist the investigation."

Logan watched an icon pop up indicating she was typing something back. It disappeared and popped back up a few times as she mulled over her response.

"I already talked to the police," she wrote. "Who are you?"

"My name is Logan Claybourne," he wrote. "I'm a private investigator assisting the police."

"I didn't know private investigators assist police," she wrote.

"I'm required to share anything I find with them," he wrote.

"Who hired you?" she wrote.

"A friend of Kenny's," he wrote back.

"Which friend?"

"I'm not at liberty to say."

"What do you want to know?" she asked.

"It would be better if I could meet with you briefly. I just need to ask a few questions and get a sense of who was involved with Kenny."

"I'm busy," she wrote. "Have the police contact me."

"Please. The police are kept very busy and I can help. Police are only going to chase this down until their leads run dry. If you can assist me, I can get further on the case. Where do you live? I'll only be a minute."

"I'm not giving you my address so you can rape and murder me," she wrote back.

"You are right to be cautious," he wrote back. "I'm assisting with the investigation. Just need to ask a couple questions."

A photo loaded onto the screen before he could finish typing his response. It was a picture of her giving him the middle finger.

"Bye fuckwad," she wrote.

"Do you know where his Corvette is?" he typed.

No response. So much for Plan A. At least she provided a workable Plan B.

Logan tapped on the photo she sent of her middle finger and opened the metadata. In the metadata, he retrieved the latitude and longitude coordinates of where the photo was taken. Logan copied those into the maps app.

It zoomed down on a house not too far away, about an hour's walk on the other side of the North Saskatchewan River.

6

The coordinates from Valerie Prince's photo pinned a little house in the Garneau neighbourhood when Logan entered them into the maps app. It took Logan on a walk along the steel beams of the High Level Bridge above the North Saskatchewan river. Scrawls of spray paint looped over the beams and over the walkway. Half way along the bridge, a bouquet of flowers hung off the high safety fence with duct tape strapped around its middle.

On the other side of the bridge, modest but well-kept homes lined winding streets. The smell of freshly cut grass greeted Logan along with fire hydrants painted to look like cartoon dogs. Roofs here and there held aloft handcrafted weathervanes shaped like roosters or airplanes.

The maps app pointed Logan toward a quaint yellow bungalow with white trim around the windows. Before walking up the steps, Logan took a walk around the block. The back alley held tidy groups of garbage bins. A dusty old Winnibego hunkered down in someone's back yard.

Logan circled back to the front and rapped on the the flyscreen door with one knuckle.

Valerie opened the door.

"Oh God," she said.

She shut the door.

"I'm sorry to bother you," said Logan, his voice raised so she could hear him through the door. "A couple questions and I'll be out of your hair."

"Can we do this outside?" she asked. "I don't need you freaking out and murdering me in my own house. Not today."

"Of course," said Logan. "I understand. This must all be very disturbing."

Valerie stepped out the door and once it was closed leaned back on it with her arms folded. She wore a purple set of nurse's scrubs and her dark hair tied back in a ponytail.

"Thanks very much," said Logan. "I'm so sorry for your loss. Truly. I'm a private investigator and I'm assisting the police. Anything you can provide would be really quite helpful."

"You mentioned," said Valerie. "Do you have a card?"

"I forgot to bring them," said Logan, feeling imaginary breast pockets on his jacket.

Valerie gave him a look as though to say, 'Well?'

"I'm really sorry to hear about your father," said Logan. "This must be very difficult for you."

"I'm not interested in discussing my family dynamic," she said. "Why don't you ask what you came here to ask?"

Logan swallowed.

"Did your dad have any enemies? Anyone have a problem with him?"

"I don't know," she said.

"Can you tell me what happened?"

"You already know, don't you?"

"In your words."

"He was shot in his house, wasn't he?"

"Did your dad ever mention anything—"

"Look," she said. "My father and I had a complicated relationship and I'm not getting into it with you. So I'm sure there's something in particular you want to ask. Let's just get to that."

"I understand," said Logan. He looked at her shoes. Sensible, sturdy-looking nurse's shoes, well worn. The laces were tied with big double knots, maybe even triple knots, and the bunny ears tucked into the sides of her shoes. The backs were battered, evidence of slipping them off and on without undoing the laces.

"I had to figure out how to do a lot of things by myself growing up," said Logan, still looking at her laces. "I had a tough childhood. Sometimes I do something kind of wrong and people around me can tell there's something different about me."

Valerie rubbed her heels together, trying to hide her feet from plain sight, but kept her eyes trained on Logan.

"Other times I think I simply react to things in a way that's not normal," Logan continued. "And that's the giveaway. I get too angry. Or I don't understand how something works - natural gas or how to fill out tax information or something like that — and then right from the get-go people know to treat me different. Put me to one side."

Valerie looked straight ahead and thought about something. Then she looked up, refusing tears attempting to emerge from under her eyes. She gave her head a little shake and let out a long breath.

"Having a tough childhood, it's like a secret identity, and I have to put a lot of work in every day trying to hide it. I wonder if maybe you kind of know what I'm talking about," said Logan. "Sorry, are you on your way to work?"

"I just got home," she said, a lump in her throat. "I work at the hospital. Nights."

Her face softened and her back slumped a bit, as if giving in.

"What do you want to know?" she said, massaging an eyebrow with the heel of her hand.

"Your father drove a blue Corvette Stingray," he said. "Any idea where it is?"

She found something about the question amusing. She gave a light snort and the beginnings of a smile appeared on her face.

"No, I'm sorry I don't," she said.

"Any places he liked to drive it to?"

"I wasn't in regular contact with my father. I couldn't say."

"You didn't talk to him much."

"A couple times a year or so."

"Your mother —"

"I never knew my mother," she said.

"You and your dad maybe not get along?"

She looked up at the sky again as though to gather strength.

"We did the best we could," she said. My father works — worked hard. And he played hard. And he didn't know how to be a dad but he loved me the best he could. On one hand, I had to raise myself but on the other he made sure I was always provided for. I never went without school supplies or toys or clothes. But the deal was, as far as growing up, I had to figure that out for myself."

She sat down on the steps and folded her arms.

"There was no one to show me how to grow up," she said. "I had to learn that the hard way."

Logan sat down next to her. She leaned away at first and then didn't mind.

"My sister and I," said Logan. "We had to figure it out too."

Valerie looked over at Logan and then away again.

"High school wasn't bad for me," said Valerie. "By then my dad was pretty open about everything. Like the women he brought over. He wasn't trying to hide it. Sometimes it worked out for me because when my friends from school wanted to party, it was easy to bring the party back to my place. My friends could experiment with alcohol. It was funny, my friends were hiding pot from their parents and I was hiding my dad's crack pipes from my friends."

A funny memory passed behind her eyes.

"Not ideal though," said Logan.

"I was always provided for," she said. "He just couldn't help being himself. And he wasn't sorry for being himself. He was just him. And I love him. But it's complicated, you dig?"

A lump filled her throat and she wiped tears out of her eyes.

"I haven't gotten any sleep," she said.

"You know the names of any of these girlfriends of his?"

"There's a rotating cast," she said. "Actually, wait. There's this one. She friended me online. I don't know why I accepted. I guess in case something happened to my dad."

She scrolled through her phone looking for the person and held it up for Logan to see.

Her name was Alexis J. She didn't post her full last name.

She had big, feathery hair. Lots of make-up. Miniskirt. Her profile picture showed her leaning over a bar with her posterior in the centre of the frame as she looked back at the camera over her shoulder.

"She's a keeper," said Valerie.

Logan asked for a closer look and scrolled down. Alexis had a few posts tagged from a strip club called The Palace.

Logan gave her phone back.

"Your dad have any other garages or places he might have parked the car?"

"You're pretty interested in that car."

She looked away and held in a smile.

"We think it might be important to the investigation," said Logan.

"For sure," she said. "I'm sorry I don't know."

There was a pause as Logan tried to think of more questions.

"Will that be all?" she asked, slapping her hands to her knees to brace herself as she stood up. Her tired eyes insisted it should be all.

She opened the door and stepped back inside.

"Yes, you've been really helpful," said Logan. "If I have any more questions, is there a good number I can get you at?"

"Nope," said Valerie, sliding inside the house. Logan turned around to see her peeking out from behind the door almost closed. "By the way, a private investigator would probably at least carry a notepad."

Logan opened his mouth to say something.

"Bye, weirdo," she said.

She shut the door and locked the deadbolt. Click.

7

The Palace strip club occupied the space on the main floor of the Coliseum Inn where Westerner Steak and Pizza used to be back when Northlands Coliseum still operated across the street on 118th Avenue and Wayne Gretzky Drive. At some point the neighbourhood got rougher, the Oilers moved downtown, and the old arena stood grey and silent. Gradually, more predatory loan shops moved into the neighbourhood, along with pawn shops and strip clubs. All the local businesses boarded up their doors, the drugs got uglier, and that was that.

A black vinyl banner saying The Palace in pink letters with pink silhouettes of women on either end covered the old Westerner sign.

A couple big boys in black leather jackets checked Logan's ID at the entrance and took their time doing it as they sized him up. One of them gave Logan his card back and tilted his head toward a second entrance door.

It was ten o'clock on Friday night, as good a time as any to find Alexis J. The DJ announced specials on high balls as college boys took their places next to construction workers and genuine old creeps along Pervert's Row at the side of the stage.

Logan took a seat at the bar. Somewhere from behind a weaponized pair of breasts in a leather bikini top a young woman asked what she could get him.

"I'm looking for someone," said Logan. "Alexis. Do you know Alexis?"

"You want something to drink?" she responded.

"Gold Star," said Logan.

The bartender grabbed a bottle out of the fridge behind her, cracked the cap off on the edge of the fridge door, and put it in front of Logan.

"Ten dollars," she said like she was issuing a parking ticket.

The air left Logan's gut and he put his last twenty dollar bill on the bar. She grabbed the money and gave him a five dollar bill and change. Logan tipped her a dollar, which she threw into a clear plastic pitcher behind the bar and disappeared before Logan could say anything else.

He turned around on his barstool and surveyed the area starting with the girl with no clothes on winding her way down a brass pole at the centre of the room. The group of college boys elbowed and punched each other in the arms.

A waitress made her way from table to table. An older man in a nice suit sat at a high top table across from a young lady who looked like she might be a dancer on her night off.

Logan saw something in the corner of his eye and when he looked to his side was startled to see Alexis sitting next to him, also taking in the room. She looked still and relaxed as though she had been sitting there for hours. Her frame was slight. She wore a black miniskirt and a black halter top. Her copper coloured hair curled down in ribbons and her button nose gave a mousey aspect to her face.

"That's Sandy," she said, looking at the dancer on stage. "She's new but she's really good."

"If she wants to be a firefighter she's going to have to learn to get down that pole a lot faster," said Logan.

"Huh?"

"Nothing."

"Someone said you asked about me," said Alexis. She asked the bartender for a glass of water and the bartender splashed some into a glass from the bar gun. "Do I know you?"

"I'm an investigator," said Logan. "I need to ask you a few questions."

The colour drained out of her face.

"I don't know anything," she said.

Logan put his hand on her arm.

"You're not in trouble. I haven't even said what it's about."

She looked around the room for an out, her right leg jittering up and down.

"Can we just talk for a minute?"

"I'm supposed to be doing stuff," she said.

"I'll just be a minute," said Logan.

She pinched the sleeve of his jacket and didn't let go the whole way as she pulled him across the club to a booth in a far corner. Bouncers standing in the wings kept their eyes on them as they walked and when they sat down, Alexis folded her arms and sulked.

"Did you know Kenny Prince?"

She rolled her eyes.

"Do you know how he died?"

She looked away from the table, almost over her shoulder.

"He got murdered, didn't he?" she said. "I don't know. Is this going to take a long time? I really have to get back."

"There's a blue Corvette Stingray," said Logan, moving his head to catch her eyes. "You know the one?"

She nodded.

"You know where it is?"

She shook her head no.

"Did Kenny ever loan it to you or anything like that?"

"No way. He loved that car," she said.

"He let you drive it around? You never took it to a friend's house?"

She forced out a laugh.

"No, nothing like that," she said. "That car was all his. He was the only one who drove it."

Bouncers in black suits slid along the back wall to get a look at their conversation.

"Is that everything?" she asked.

"Well, no," said Logan. "Do you know what happened?"

"Nope," she said. "Anything else?"

"Who might have done this? Do you know?"

"No idea," she said, her arms hugging tight around her middle. She opened her eyes wide and looked him plainly in the face. "Is that everything?"

She pushed her chair back.

"No, that's not everything," Logan barked at her. The bouncers along the wall took sudden interest and took a step forward. Alexis gave them a look that told them to stand down. Logan made a point of smiling.

"That's not everything," he said with a forced smirk on his face. "Where were you when it happened?"

She thought about her answer.

"I was here at the club," she said. "Look, I really have to get back to work."

"Stop," said Logan. She stood up at the table but didn't move and looked down at him.

A man with slicked back hair and a suit the colour of red wine appeared from around a corner. He put his arm around Alexis.

"Everything alright?" he asked.

She nodded.

"I think the girls in the back need help with something," he said, and gave her a smack on the ass.

The man looked Logan up and down.

"What are you doing here?"

"Talking," said Logan.

"Why don't you get another beer or something?" he said.

He escorted Alexis away with his hand flat against her back. The only way back to the bar was around the front of the stage. Logan followed close behind. When they reached the bar the guy in the suit faded into a back wall where he leaned into the ear of one of the bouncers with some kind of instruction.

Alexis asked for another glass of water. The bartender filled up a glass.

"A man is dead," said Logan. "I just want to talk."

"I can't talk right now," she said.

"Are you getting a beer or what, pal?" asked the bartender.

"Let me buy you breakfast," said Logan.

Alexis froze.

"Tomorrow, at the Take Five," Logan insisted.

"I work late," she said.

"Noon, tomorrow, at the Take Five," said Logan.

"Hey, bud, beer?"

"Sunday at noon," said Alexis.

"Sunday, noon, at the Take Five," Logan repeated at her. Alexis made eye contact and nodded as another girl pulled her away behind the black curtain.

A bouncer stepped close enough to Logan he could smell his body odour and made no other effort to give Logan any space. Logan sneered at him. The bouncer squared up to Logan and motioned with his hands to try him. Logan brushed past him and pushed his way out the front door.

The fresh air outside halted Logan as he walked. He breathed it in deeply and then walked for an hour along the avenue. It was Friday night and the traffic jumped along with plenty of hooting and hollering. Working girls shouted at drunks across the street. Young tough guys wavered on their bicycles through the traffic.

Logan sent a text message to Ricky.

"You said you had some other jobs? The Corvette might take a while."

"Ya," came the response. "Get the truck. I'll text you the address in the morning."

Logan walked his way down 118th Avenue, past the bleeting traffic, past the sex workers heckling drunks on the other side of the street, past old homeless men picking bottles out of garbage cans, past people spasming and convulsing on the sidewalk from whatever mixture of chemicals was going around these days.

When Logan arrived at Champion City Pawn he made his way to the back lot. The pitbulls, Trixie and Dixie, bounded to the fence barking and slobbering. Logan made kissy noises at them as he opened the fence. They hopped up on his legs and scurried around.

"No treats today," said Logan. "Sorry."

The lot held an assortment of vehicles in various states of depreciation. Some of them Logan had repossessed. Others Ricky acquired in sideways business deals and they rested mid-way through the process of being flipped somewhere else. A Volvo up on blocks. An F-150 with the front end smashed in. A late 90s Cadillac collecting dust.

At the centre of the lot stood Sal. Sal was Ricky's tow truck — a 1982 Dodge Power Wagon that was more rust than truck. It had a large tow lift on the back operated with levers on the side. In faded white lettering on the grey doors it read 'Sal's Auto Repair' with a barely legible phone number. Rust ate at the edges of the door and it creaked as Logan opened it.

A cloud of dark smoke belched out the back end as he started the engine and Sal shook to life. He kept his feet on the pedals. Rust had eaten away at a lot of the floor, the road visible through the holes. He wrestled the gear shift into first. The gears clanked and the chassis moaned as he rolled out of the lot.

He locked the gate behind him and drove the tow truck to his apartment building so the next morning he could get up and go.

On Saturday morning, Logan drank some coffee and ate his last samosa. He shuffled cards until he was awake, then made his way downstairs and got in the truck.

A text message came in from Ricky with a photo of the contract. A minivan to a signee by the name of Desiree Klassen at an apartment about ten blocks up the avenue.

"On my way," Logan texted back.

The tow truck shuddered and bounced down the street until he came upon a three-floor apartment building called the Ambassador. One of the numbers was missing from the address on the front wall and jaundiced grass spread out across the lawn.

The purple minivan was parked out front with both the rear hatchback and the side door open. A cooler and a cardboard box sat on the lawn. Logan pulled in front of the van, turned his hazard lights on, and reversed until the tow bar nudged the van's front tires.

A young woman in grey sweatpants and a white tank top kicked open the front door of the apartment building while carrying a cardboard box in front of her. She made it to the sidewalk before noticing Logan and the tow truck and sat down on the cooler and buried her face in her hands.

"Fuck," she said. "Just take it. Might as well."

Two children, a boy and a girl, struggled to open the front door of the apartment as they each carried one end of a vacuum cleaner. The door closed on the older girl first as she hobbled backward, holding the bottom end of the vacuum. She braced the door with her body and shoved it back. The door closed again on the middle of the vacuum, pinching it in place. After some thinking, the girl held on to her end of the vacuum and kicked the door so it swung open long enough to slam again on her little brother who carried the handle end of the vacuum. He started to cry but looked at his mom and saw the stranger with the tow truck, assessed the situation, and sucked on his bottom lip to keep quiet.

"Look mom," the girl said. "We're helping."

"Good job, sweetie," said their mom. She wiped her hands down the side of her face. "Don't work too hard. I think we don't even have a van anymore so it really doesn't matter."

"What do you mean?" asked the girl.

"Nothing," said mom. "I don't know."

"Moving?" asked Logan.

"That's the idea," she said. "But my piece of shit landlord won't give me my damage deposit!"

She yelled it loud enough for the whole block to hear. The kids lugged the vacuum into the back of the van and came around to sit next to their mom.

"It's OK," said the girl, leaning her head on her mom's shoulder. "Everything will be alright."

"Thanks sweetie," said her mom. She leaned her head on her daughter's head.

The girl stood up again and wagged a finger at her brother.

"Come on, Brody," she said. "There's more work to do."

She pulled her brother's wrist and they waddled back inside the apartment building.

"I'm supposed to take the van," said Logan.

"I kind of figured," she said. "Go ahead. I'm basically fucking homeless anyway."

"He won't give you your damage deposit?"

"He says it's for damages, which is bullshit," she said. "The kids made some art on the wall because of course they did. They're kids. I don't think that's twelve hundred dollars worth of damage though. You're taking the van anyway. Fuck it. We'll leave all my shit here and walk to the women's shelter."

The kids pushed their way through the door again, both walking backwards and dragging garbage bags full of clothes.

"Don't work too hard, sweetie," Desiree called to her daughter.

"Don't worry about it," said Logan. "Get out of here."

"Aren't you supposed to take the van?"

"I didn't see you. Ricky will have to sell this to a collections agency though. It'll hit your credit pretty hard."

"Do I look like someone who can afford to care about their credit?"

Logan walked back to the truck and rolled it away from her front tires. Desiree remained seated on the cooler, watching Logan move the truck like it was some faraway thing or an irrelevant video on her phone. He got out and stepped over to the levers on the side, behind the driver's seat, lifted the tow bar back into place.

He gave one last look to Desiree. Her tired face gave no expression. Logan got in and drove away around the block.

The phone in his pocket rang. He pulled into the parking lot of a skating rink. It was Ricky on the phone.

"You get the van?"

"She wasn't there."

"What do you mean she wasn't there?"

"She skipped. Place was empty."

Ricky cursed and Logan could hear him pacing as they hung up. Then he drove the truck back to the shop.

8

The odds your car will be stolen are three in one thousand. About the same as being dealt a suited Ace-King.

Are the odds assigned to you the day you are born? Or do the odds in life refresh every day, perhaps reordering themselves at the stroke of midnight? Where do the numbers go? Are we reborn anew each day with refreshed odds? Or are the numbers set in motion long before us and the forces of debt and scarcity simply grind us into dust over time? If we could see the numbers and the alignment of the stars, could we cheat them?

Logan spent the morning sitting at the dinner table shuffling cards. Meditating. The great ordering and re-ordering of things.

At ten-thirty he sent a message to Alexis.

"You still good to meet at noon at the Take Five?"

He resumed shuffling cards and over the next hour didn't get a response. Top card to second position. Riffle. Second card to third position, top card to second position. Riffle.

At twenty to twelve Logan put the cards down and put on his jacket. On his way out the door he sent another message to Alexis.

"I'm on my way to the Take Five. I'll see you there."

Along the avenue, even the stores that were open looked closed. Their dark windows showed no movement inside. At an intersection a young woman with a dirty face and dirty clothes contorted and spasmed as some chemical worked its way through her body.

The walk took him past The Palace strip club, along an overpass above Wayne Gretzky Drive, and into the next community of Bellvue.

The Take Five diner jutted out at the end of a strip mall next to a dollar store, a nail salon, and a liquor store.

It was almost noon and Logan sent another message to Alexis.

"Here," it read.

He sat at a table in the back corner and watched people pass by out the window for half an hour when a message came back from Alexis.

"OMG, I'm so sorry," it read. "Are you still there?"

"Yup," Logan responded.

"I'm running late," she wrote back. "Do you still want to meet up?"

"No problem," said Logan. "I can wait."

There was a pause.

"On my way," she wrote.

An older woman with an Eastern European accent came around and asked Logan if he wanted any food and scowled when he said he was waiting for someone.

The Take Five still hung on to a lazy atmosphere most restaurants don't have time for these days. They weren't in a hurry to make any money. Maybe their rent was cheap. Maybe they owned the property. But whereas these days most places churned people through the cash register and back out the door at an industrial pace, the Take Five showed no such gumption. It wasn't as though the Take Five was happy to let people sit around. It was more like they didn't want customers in the first place.

The woman disappeared into the back and didn't emerge again for another twenty minutes, and only then because a man rang the bell at the cash register wanting to buy some doughnuts.

At around one o'clock, Alexis walked in the door. She looked small, all bundled up in sweatpants and a hoodie far too large for her. She seemed to sense where Logan was sitting without ever looking up at him and drifted across the diner to his table.

The waitress came over, dumped a couple menus on the table, turned over the coffee mug in front of Alexis and poured coffee into it without anyone saying anything.

"Sorry, I got caught up," said Alexis.

"No problem," said Logan.

"So who are you again?" she asked. "Are you a cop?"

"No," said Logan. "I'm a private investigator. I've been hired by a another party to look into this. You're not in any trouble. I just want to talk and when we're done, I never even met you."

"I have enough problems without cops all up in my shit," she said.

"For sure," said Logan.

"What if a cop asks you about me?"

"I have a really bad memory," said Logan. "I never even heard of you."

Her hands slipped out of her sleeves to empty three creamer packets into her coffee and she poured sugar into it for several long Mississippis. Then her hands disappeared back inside her sleeves and she wrapped them both around the coffee mug.

"I guess it doesn't matter," she said. "It's not like we did anything bad. Not that bad, anyway."

Logan leaned in and lowered his voice.

"Can you tell me what happened?"

She closed her eyes. Her leg jittered under the table.

"There was a bunch of us there," she said, and shook her head as in disbelief of everything.

"We were just having a good time. Kenny liked it when everyone was in the hot tub. Which is — whatever."

The waitress came back and asked if they wanted something to eat. Her tone insisted they should, on account that Logan had been sitting there for almost a couple hours.

Logan and Alexis scanned the menus.

"Could I have the raspberry pancakes with lots of whip cream, bacon and sausage, and two poached eggs — poached medium, and white toast?"

The old woman held her gaze on Alexis, registering her order without writing it down. Then she turned to Logan.

"I'll just have another coffee, thanks," said Logan.

"You're not hungry?" asked Alexis.

"I already ate."

The waitress turned her nose up at Logan and walked away into the back.

"Who else was there?" asked Logan.

"Some friends of mine," said Alexis. "Breanne, Tannis, and Michelle. They didn't know Kenny as well as me, but they make it fun. Kenny liked to feel like a big man and made it worth their while. And he liked to party. There was plenty of booze for everyone when they arrived. Cocaine. We all fool around in the hot tub. Try to get Kenny so drunk he passes out as soon as possible. Same as usual. But he was a tank. They left before anything happened."

"What happened?"

"I don't even know," she said, her throat clenching up. "I was taking a shower. When I got out of the shower I heard a fight. At first I was going to go out to help break it up, but they were really going at it. It wasn't like drunk guys being macho at the bar. They were fucking up the whole house. And I was standing there naked, dripping wet. And Kenny was a big guy. He could do some damage if he wanted to. But then the fighting stopped. And then there was a gun shot. Twice. Like, 'bang' and then, 'bang'. I bit my hand to keep from screaming. And I got dressed and I sat in the bathroom for an hour. I heard the other guy leave. But I was so scared I sat in the bathroom for an hour until I was sure."

"That's awful, I'm sorry," said Logan. "You heard the other guy leave? Did he take the Corvette?"

She nodded yes.

"I could hear him start it. It's hard to miss. Sounds like a jet engine when it's going. And the Corvette was definitely there when I got there in the afternoon and it wasn't there when I left."

"And you left shortly after that?"

"Yeah, like an hour after that I came out of the bathroom. It was quiet. And when I saw Kenny in the living room —"

She turned to the side with tears in her eyes and stared down at the floor.

"It's OK," said Logan.

"I just ran," she said.

Logan sipped his coffee and gave Alexis time to collect herself. The waitress returned with Alexis' food and placed it in front of her. Alexis' eyes lit up. The waitress took a short trip to the coffee station and returned to top up their cups. She asked if everything was fine and Logan and Alexis confirmed it was.

Alexis poured a thick blanket of syrup over everything on her plate and dove into her food like she hadn't eaten in days.

"Did Kenny make any enemies with his business?"

She chewed as she thought about the question and shrugged.

"I don't think so."

"Did he own those sump trucks?"

"Yeah," she said, and nodded.

"How many trucks did he own?"

"Just the two, I'm pretty sure. Dennis drove the other one."

Alexis' face was about four inches away from her plate as she sopped up some syrup with a whipped cream-covered wad of pancake and shoved it in her mouth.

"Dennis? Who's Dennis?"

She laughed at the question and pressed a finger to her lips to keep food from spraying out.

"Dennis is harmless," she said. "He lives in a bus out at Rusty's RV Park. Do you know it?"

"I think so. Out west."

She nodded and shoveled more pancake in her mouth before the previous wad was dispatched down her throat.

"That's where they park the trucks."

"Could the Corvette be out there, do you think?"

She screwed up her mouth and hummed a doubtful note.

"You could check," she said.

"OK, but I'd appreciate it if you would take your time with this question," said Logan. "Think back. Did Kenny have any other enemies? Anyone that would want to hurt Kenny?"

Alexis looked up at the ceiling as she munched her food.

"No," she said. "Everybody loved Kenny. He was really fun."

Logan let the question linger.

"Unless Talia counts," she said into her plate, her cheek bulging as she chewed. She lifted her eyebrows as she thought about it. "She fucking hated Kenny."

"Talia? Who's Talia?" asked Logan.

"This uptight bitch who lived in the building next door to Kenny's house," she said. "She and Kenny would get in arguments all the time. They were so funny."

Alexis laughed.

"What kind of funny?"

Alexis snorted from laughter as she remembered something.

"One time she was yelling at us from her balcony. About the noise or something, I don't know. And Kenny stood up on the edge of his hot tub. He was just in a leather Speedo and a cowboy hat. He was carrying a champagne bottle in one hand and he made the jerking off motion at her with the other. The rest of us took our tops off and passed a joint around and waved at her."

"I bet she loved that," said Logan.

Alexis' gaze drifted off into the distance as she lost herself in the memory, a smile stretching across her face.

"What was she upset about the most do you think? All the partying?"

"She's upset she's a snaggle-toothed bitch, I think," said Alexis. "Everything annoyed her. He couldn't leave the house without making her head spin."

"Maybe she was offended by drug use?" said Logan.

"She was offended by her own vagina," said Alexis. She shrugged. "We partied, sure. I don't know if that's enough reason for her to assassinate Kenny, if that's what you mean. Bodkins. That's her last name. Talia Bodkins."

She said Talia's name with a nasally, uptight tone.

"What else do you know about Talia?" asked Logan.

"I don't know," said Alexis. "She's on her condo board or something. You should totally get the police after her. That would be hilarious."

"I'll see what I can do."

Alexis guzzled down some coffee and dragged more pancakes around her plate with her fork.

"Feels stupid I have to sit here and tell you all about my life and I don't even know you," she said.

"What do you want to know?"

She thought about it.

"Do you have a girlfriend?" she asked.

"That's a little forward," Logan responded.

"Don't get excited," said Alexis. "I'm not looking."

"No," said Logan. "I don't have a girlfriend."

"Why not?"

"I guess the right girl hasn't come along."

"That's not a reason," she said. "What is it? Are you a weirdo? Just broke up with someone? Divorced? Alcoholic?"

"I guess I'm just fine being by myself," said Logan.

"That could be either hot or weird," she said. "Depending."

"What else do you want to know?"

She looked up and pointed at him with her fork.

"Why does your mouth do that thing?"

"What thing do I do with my mouth?"

"You pucker your lips when you're trying to be cool."

"I didn't know I was doing that."

She shrugged.

"Do you do drugs?"

"Not really," he said. "I've smoked pot here and there. Experimented with a couple other things. I don't like feeling not in control of myself though."

That answer seemed to satisfy her and her attention returned to her plate.

"Did Kenny get mixed up with any drug problems?" Logan asked. "Any drug dealers mad at him?"

She thought about it.

"No," she said. "He only goes through the one guy as far as I know. They get along fine."

"I think I'd like to talk to him," said Logan. "Can you introduce me?"

"I don't know," she said. "It's awkward."

"I'll be cool," said Logan. "Just want to see if they have any leads."

She sulked and didn't move. She thought about it and gave in and pulled a cell phone out from somewhere within the heaping hoodie she was in.

"Hey, what are you doing?" Alexis asked into the phone. "I have someone who wants to talk to you— Probably not— About Kenny— No, he's not a cop— Because he doesn't seem like a cop— He's a private investigator— I don't because he doesn't give off cop vibes— He's just a guy— His name's Logan— What's your last name again?"

"Claybourne," said Logan.

"Logan Claybourne," she said into the phone again. "OK."

She hung up.

"He said he'd call back in a minute," she said.

They sipped coffee and looked out the window while they waited. Soon enough he called back.

"Hello?" she asked. "Uh huh. Uh huh. OK."

She hung up.

"He says to meet him in Goldsworthy Park," she said. "We can walk it."

"Right now?" asked Logan.

"Yeah, right now," she said. "When else?"

Alexis' little legs moved pretty quick and Logan almost struggled to keep up as he followed her into a neighbourhood of low-income brick apartment buildings that kept to themselves, all dark and quiet. Goldsworthy Park was a quarter-acre of dead grass surrounded by broken chain link fence, snipped in places and bent and falling off the frame.

"He'll be over there," she said, pointing to the other side of the park. Logan kept his eyes on the ground to avoid needles, broken glass and dog shit. When they reached the other side, they stood at a bus stop and waited.

The wind whipped by and they dug their hands into their pockets and hunched their shoulders up by their ears until a silver Acura slid its way down the street and parked a block ahead from where they were standing.

"That's him," she said, and touched Logan's lower back to push him along. "That's BB."

"BB?"

She nodded and stayed at the bus stop and shooed him along with her hand. Logan walked over and crouched down to look in the passenger side window. The man inside had full-sleeve tattoos on his arms and gold flashed across all his bottom teeth. He leered back at Logan out the side of his eye.

"How's it going?" asked Logan.

BB didn't say anything but only looked Logan up and down and gave a nod with an upward tick of his head.

"A friend of Kenny's asked me to look around," said Logan. "Try to figure out what happened."

"Sure, sure," said BB.

"I'm sorry. I'm told Kenny was a great guy."

"Kenny was a piece of shit," he said. "But I liked him."

"Do you know what happened?"

"I heard what happened," he said. "It's not good."

"You heard who might have done this?"

BB looked around and was distracted by a hollowed out phone booth across the street. The phone was ripped out a lifetime ago and graffiti splashed over the inside walls.

"Get in," he said.

Logan got into the passenger side of the very clean Acura, the black dashboard glistening with fresh Armour All.

"Where you from Logan?"

"Around here."

"A friend of Kenny's asked you to look around?"

"That's right."

"What friend?"

"They want to keep it private. You wouldn't know them."

"I guess not."

"What do you think happened to Kenny?" asked BB.

"It's a bit of a mystery. I was hoping you might have heard a rumor or two."

"Well, I haven't," said BB. "And normally I do with this kind of thing, you know what I mean? I want to talk about this some more," said BB. "You need to do me a favour though."

"What kind of favour?"

"Come here for a sec."

BB got out of the Acura and Logan did too. BB walked around the front of the car and leaned in close to Logan.

"I'm going to talk to some guys over there," he said, motioning with his elbow toward the phone booth. Logan didn't see anyone. "Just stand here and try to look like a hard motherfucker."

He grabbed Logan's jacket with both hands and straightened it with a sharp tug. He looked Logan in the eye and stood erect with his chest puffed out so Logan would do the same.

Logan mumbled something sort of like an 'OK.'

BB crossed the road and when he reached the phone booth two shadowy men appeared from nowhere, seemingly from the cracks in the sidewalk. BB ducked into the phone booth with one of the men while the other draped himself over the telephone booth doorway, reaching up to hang off the top of the door frame. Logan stood like a bouncer, his back straight, and loosely held his right wrist in his left hand in front of him.

The guys in the phone booth hunched over together to look at something. Logan glanced back at the bus stop. Alexis was gone. The men in the phone booth talked and their voices grew louder and heated. They took turns barking at each other. It reached a boiling point and then BB shouted something and directed their attention at Logan.

BB and the other guy inside poked their head out to look at Logan and the big guy turned away from the phone booth to look over at Logan as well. Logan stood straight with a sour expression on his face. The three faces ducked back into the phone booth, their matter apparently resolved. They concluded their transaction and the two men stepped away from the booth. They both stopped to look back across the street to size up Logan one more time, and then slipped back into the shadows along the walls.

"Get in," said BB as he crossed the street back to the car. Logan got into the passenger seat and BB sped off, weaving in and out between the other cars on the road. He was relaxed in the driver's seat. Logan leaned back but his right hand gripped the side of his seat tightly.

"What was that about?" asked Logan.

"I told them they were going down a very dark path if they planned on crossing you. I'm glad it worked because I don't know what plan B was going to be if it didn't."

"OK."

"You're looking for that Stingray, ain't you?" asked BB.

"How'd you know?"

BB smiled.

"I don't know where it is," he said.

"Have you heard anything at all?" asked Logan.

"No," he said.

He shifted gears well. Lightly. Matter-of-factly. The paddle shifters behind the wheel cover up a lot of mistakes for novice drivers compared to the old stick shift, but BB knew what he was doing, upshifting and downshifting right on cue to a rhythm under the car that carried them down the street without a stutter or missed beat.

"I don't know what Kenny got himself into," said BB. "But it's weird. It's not regular hood shit. Usually when someone gets offed it's because they ripped someone off or there's a grudge everybody knows about. Even if people don't know exactly who did it, they still have a pretty good idea. You dig? This, there's nothing."

He took a ramp onto the freeway.

"Where do you live?" he said. "I'll give you a ride."

Logan gave his address. BB sliced through the traffic as he changed lanes.

"What have you heard?" asked BB.

"He was shot on his couch," said Logan. "Someone stuck a QR code sticker on the wall above him. That mean anything to you?"

BB thought about it.

"It's weird," he said. "It's mechanical."

"How do you mean?"

"It's a different world," he said. "If the QR code has something to do with the murder, it's not exactly a crime of passion, is it? It's some Terminator robot shit. Nothing means anything anymore."

The road curved into the sun. BB lowered the visor and squinted through the windshield.

"Like with music," he said. "Used to be you'd go out and find something you like. Now it's an algorithm telling you what you like and fire-hosing you with it. Internet tells you what news you want. Like, it figures out your brain and your personality. It's like we're still human but not as human as we used to be. Now we're part human, part equations."

"I think I know what you mean," said Logan. "Casinos don't look how they used to. Less and less table games. More and more VLTs fill the floor where people just touch a button and wait for their numbers to come up."

"Folks don't want all the window dressing on their lives anymore," said BB. "It's all 'get to the point.'"

"We all want the big algorithm to grind it all down, play the numbers out faster to whatever end it is we're headed for."

"Cops are probably looking for someone with a motive because their instinct is to find meaning in it," said BB. "Maybe that's where they're going wrong."

They thought about it a while until BB pulled off the main road to hide amongst the residential streets. Logan gave him directions to his apartment building. They made their way around rundown homes. They came upon a mail carrier in a reflective vest walking from house to house, big bags hanging off either side of him. BB slowed down.

"These motherfuckers," said BB, nodding toward the mail carrier. He whistled and sorted through a handful of mail as he came away from someone's door onto the sidewalk. BB rolled down the passenger side window and leaned over the middle console to shout at him.

"Pretty hard to compete against the new generation of drug dealers," BB yelled at the confused-looking mail carrier. "Asshole!"

BB rolled the window back up.

"These days on the dark web people can get whatever they want mail order," he said. "Hell, you don't even need the dark web for some of this shit. You can get a doctor in Texas to prescribe you Xanax, and a pharmacy in Pittsburgh will mail it to you. And this army of government paid drug dealers will walk it right up to your front door. And on the dark web you can get anything. Acid. Fentanyl. You name it. It's hard for your old fashioned drug dealer to make an honest living anymore."

He double parked outside Logan's apartment.

"Check this out," said BB. He pulled out his phone and pulled up some social media. He scrolled through the photos for Logan to see. Each photo showed some dopey looking well-to-do kid. They wore name brand clothes that looked slightly out of place on them. They had short, spiked hair and wore expensive looking golf visors, Oakley sunglasses, and jackets that looked like they belonged on rap stars more than a skinny white kid in the suburbs.

In all the photos they posed with bowls of white pills.

"Xanax," said BB. "These kids call themselves the 420 Xanax Mafia. Ain't that the stupidest shit you ever heard in your life? They hack people's social media accounts and sell the usernames."

"There good money in that?" asked Logan.

"Enough to get fucked up and play video games all day as far as I can tell," said BB. "They make shitty rap songs about how they can't get laid. But that's my point. Nobody wants to do a little blow and party anymore. These kids just mail order drugs from the dark web and play Call of Duty. You dig? It's like they're organisms kept captive by the internet - the machine. What's a friendly neighbourhood drug dealer to do?"

The traffic piled up behind him and a couple cars honked.

"Thanks for the ride," said Logan, and he got out of the car. "Keep it real, Sherlock," said BB and he sped away.

9

The next morning, Logan sat up on his mattress on the floor. A light rain pattered at the windows. He picked up a deck of cards that lay next to the bed and shuffled. He held half the deck in each hand and riffled them together, alternating the cards from each hand one for one as evenly as he could. Once both sides meshed together, he arched them into a bridge and let them waterfall into a tidy stack.

If you shuffle a deck of cards perfectly, with the deck cut into twenty-six cards in each hand and each card perfectly interleaved one for one from each hand, then it only takes eight perfect shuffles for the deck to return to its original order. That is, if you leave the same top card on top. It's called a Faro shuffle.

If you evenly shuffle in the top cards, then it takes twenty-six perfect shuffles to reverse the order of the deck, and twenty-six more to return to its original order.

The first kind of Faro shuffle is called an in-shuffle. The other is called an out-shuffle. Someone who is adept at both Faro shuffles can decide where in the deck they would like to place the top card if they can express that position as a binary number.

So if you want six cards above your Ace, six is expressed in binary as 0110. You do an out-shuffle for each zero and an in-shuffle for each one. So to get six cards stacked on top of our Ace it would be out-shuffle, in-shuffle, in-shuffle, out-shuffle.

But of course, anyone this good at shuffling doesn't need to study radix values and Artin's conjecture of primitive roots to get an Ace to fall in the sixth position when good old slight-of-hand will do. It was just the kind of thing Logan liked to think about.

Most people at a dining table poker game shuffle cards like cavemen. And that's the first rule of card shuffling — always appear as though you shuffle the cards only as well as the people around you and not any better.

If they drop a card, you drop a card. If their shuffle gets cluttered up, you jam the cards together in your hands like you're balling up a wad of dough.

To do otherwise alerts people to the fact that it's no longer a game of chance.

Logan could not yet do perfect Faro shuffles, but the practice was relaxing. He wasn't particularly eager to get to the point where he could perform perfect Faro shuffles. It was enough to get into a Zen state of analyzing the smallest touches of his fingertips in every failed Faro shuffle.

He breathed in time with the riffling cards and sensed within himself his pulse slowing down and his breaths deepening.

Logan thought about the day Kenny Prince was killed and tried to imagine what happened.

Kenny had a small party. Brought some ladies from the strip club home. They partied with cocaine and booze and hung out in the hot tub and listened to old heavy metal music.

Eventually the drugs ran out and the girls went home, or on to the next party.

Alexis stayed around because she was Kenny's main squeeze.

They had some more drinks. Maybe they're wasted by that point. Maybe they have sex.

Alexis goes to the washroom to shower and while she's in there she hears a man enter the premises. She hears them shouting and fighting.

It's especially violent. She hides in the washroom.

Kenny seemed like a big guy. If he was subdued it must have been with a weapon, but his inebriation set him back too. Maybe brass knuckles if they were rolling around and fighting. A bat would have been too clumsy at close range. Kenny was in a daze. The fight rolls into the living room. Then a few more blows and Kenny's on the couch. Then the killer pulls out a gun. Shoots Kenny twice. Puts a QR Code on the wall above Kenny's dead body. Why? Scans the QR Code with his phone. To trigger something. Perhaps to report the kill or the location of the body. To who? Grabs Kenny's keys. Walks out the front door. Drives away in the Corvette.

Was Kenny murdered for the Corvette? It had to have been about more than the car. If someone wanted the car, they could have just gotten Kenny drunk and taken the car. They didn't need to blow his head off. And the QR Code implied a degree of sophistication far beyond the merits of a 1976 Stingray.

Where were the neighbors? It was late so most people were asleep. There were two big buildings on either side. Someone must have seen something. Maybe they were used to strange noises coming out of Kenny's place and thought nothing of it.

Alexis mentioned his neighbour Talia Bodkins. Seemed like she kept close tabs on Kenny's comings and goings.

Logan pulled the cellphone off the charger next to him and searched her name on the internet. It wasn't long before he got a hit.

A website for the Body, Mind, and Soul Wellness Gathering named her as vice president of sales.

The ten-day convention took place once a year at the Northlands Convention Centre and brought in hundreds of New Age gurus, yoga instructors, and motivational speakers who flogged all manner of crystals, herbal creams, prayer candles, deionized water, meditation doctrines, and mostly their own personality cult. Every year the convention packed in thousands of locals. Some came to feel healthy for a weekend. Some came to elevate their clout in the New Age health scene. And many others simply came to see something different and take a litmus test on modern eccentricity. Just about everybody left with a piece of quartz, a scented candle, or a bottle of kombucha.

Logan had never been to the Body, Mind, and Soul Wellness Gathering but he had played poker at the Northlands Casino adjoined to the convention centre while the event happened. Some of the less enlightened participants stumbled into the casino for drinks after the convention closed to reflect on the day and try to get laid.

He phoned the number on the website. A receptionist answered. Logan asked for Talia and got put through to her voicemail.

"I'm sorry I can't take your call," she said on her voicemail. Her voice was chipper, as would be expected from the VP of sales of anything. But there was also hypnotic relaxedness to it, which Logan imagined must come from doing business with that New Age spiritual scene. And on top of that, there was a velvety quality to it, like the last sip of a stiff drink.

"Hello Ms. Bodkins, my name is Logan Claybourne," he said. He tried to sound like a cop but embarrassed himself with his results. "I'm assisting with the investigation into an incident that happened near your building. I was hoping to ask you a few questions. If you could please return my call as soon as possible, I'd appreciate it."

He gave his number and hung up.

He got up and made toast and coffee for breakfast. Another deck of cards lay on the counter, these ones with white patches worn through the pattern on the backs from where Logan had practiced spinning techniques. He picked it up and resumed shuffling. Nothing fancy. He riffled and shucked, and shucked and riffled, in a simple, repetitive manner for the rhythm if nothing else.

He thought about Alexis standing naked in the bathroom and listening to the two gun blasts that killed Kenny. How loud would that have been?

The phone rang. The caller ID said 'Body, Mind, and Soul.'

"Claybourne," he answered.

It was Talia Bodkins.

"You said you had some questions for me?" she said.

He could hear the smile stretched across her face, like she found everything perfectly amusing.

Logan asked if he could come see her at her office that afternoon. She said that would be fine.

"Can't we just take care of this over the phone?" she asked. "I don't really have any information. I don't want you to waste your time."

Interviewing her over the phone wouldn't do. She could say anything she wanted over the phone and Logan would still be at home, flipping cards around, no further ahead. You can learn a lot about a person by sitting in the same room as them. Their life story, sometimes. They don't need to say a word.

Besides, the Stingray had to be parked somewhere. It didn't hurt to cross one more street off the list.

"I'll just be a minute," he said.

10

The 122 bus shuttled Logan to a block of drab office buildings at the edge of an industrial park. Across the street, semi-trucks loaded out of a warehouse. Workers in reflective clothing lined up heavy machinery along the side of the road, preparing to take them to a job site somewhere.

The offices of the Body, Mind and Soul Wellness Gathering occupied the second floor of a two-floor building. A lone fern decorated the lobby on the main floor and Logan climbed the stairs to the second floor.

The reception desk sat in front of a semi-opaque glass wall with spacious cubicles partly visible behind it.

A girl with thick rimmed glasses and cute blue blazer and a bow tie typed away and pretended not to notice Logan until he was right in front of her. Logan said he had an appointment with Talia Bodkins.

She asked him his name and scanned his face as he answered. She nodded and said she would let Talia know he was there and typed into her laptop without looking up at him again.

Logan sat down on the velvet couch in the small waiting space. Next to him a large bookshelf extended from the wall and partitioned off the hallway space that led toward the cubicles and office spaces. A smattering of attractive books and antique toys adorned the shelves. Logan saw books on post-modern architecture, the history of punk rock concert posters, and vegan recipes. A rolled up yoga mat stuck out from one of the cubby spaces. Electronic music emanated softly from somewhere.

A door to an office opened at the end of the hall. Voices spoke tersely from inside the office.

"I assure you, Ms. Bodkins, we will be following up and we will take the matter before the courts if need be," a man's voice said.

Two squat men in suits came out of the office, flustered and red-faced, both carrying briefcases. A young woman with short hair and a long, flowing blazer followed behind them.

"If you're going to audit me, please have the courtesy of knowing applicable tax laws first," she said.

One of the men spun on his heel to speak back at her.

"You're not declaring your whole operation," he said, before resuming course back toward the reception area.

"Those are contract positions," she said, shooing them along with a hawk-like stare at their backs.

"We will be pursuing this in its entirety," the other man said as they opened the door to leave.

"Tell the minister I say 'Hi.' OK, buh bye," she said, and closed the door after them.

The girl at reception stood at attention.

Talia walked over to her and leaned over the desk to speak to her.

"The next time you tell them I'm here, you're fired, OK? If they come back, you tell them I'm in Vancouver. They can sit on the couch all day long for all I care." Talia looked Logan up and down out of the side of her eye. "Is there a homeless man on our couch?"

"That's Detective Claybourne," said the receptionist. Her eyes smiled. Talia ran her fingers through her hair and scratched her head then took a deep breath.

"Well this ought to be rich," she said. She turned to walk back to her office and raised her right hand and waved for him to follow with all four fingers.

"Come," she said, and Logan followed her down the hall.

They sat down at her desk where a large window behind her overlooked several blocks of warehouses.

"I'm sorry, did you say you were a police inspector?" she said.

"I'm a private investigator assisting with the case," said Logan.

"Adorable," said Talia. "Can we make this quick? I'm busy and I don't think there's much I can help you with."

Logan pulled a notepad out of his pocket.

"I'm just going to take some notes," he said, holding it up.

"What do you want to know?"

"I don't know," said Logan. "Did you kill him?"

"Excuse me?"

She laughed a distinct nasally sort of laugh that made her nose pinch in on itself.

"Did you kill your neighbour Mr. Prince?" asked Logan.

"No," she said. "I didn't."

"Are you sure?"

"Positive," she said.

"Well then, who did kill him?"

"I'm sorry, I don't know," she said, a smile breaking through.

"Did you take his car?"

"No, sorry," she said.

"You're being rather uncooperative," said Logan.

"I'm not uncooperative," she said. "I'm honest."

"This is a nice office," said Logan, leaning back and stretching out.

"Were you expecting something else?"

"Maybe more hippies. More pot," said Logan.

"Some of our clients might be a little out there but we're a business like any other. I have some edible samples in my desk, though, if you want some."

"I'll be alright," he said. "Seriously though, you don't know where that car is do you? The blue Corvette?"

She laughed, her nose pinching in on itself and she covered her mouth with her hand.

"Is the car important to your investigation?" she asked.

"We think it might be," said Logan.

"Is it missing? Thank God. I hope someone drove that car off the face of the Earth," she said. "I hate that car."

Logan didn't say anything and let her continue.

"He used to sit in that car and just rev the engine in the middle of the night."

"Just to listen to it?"

"I'm almost positive he did it only to piss me off but it's hard to say," she said. "It would be two in the morning and he would stumble over to the car drunk and would rev the engine as high as it would go. It sounded like a plane landing. And then he would go back in the house."

"Sounds like you guys were the best of friends."

"BFF's for sure," said Talia. "He spent the better part of every weekend trying to piss me off and it worked."

"Why do you think he did that?"

"He didn't like me and I didn't like him," said Talia.

"I guess it got past the point where you couldn't look away?"

"You couldn't not see it," said Talia. Redness flushed around her cheeks and her temples. "He was a blight on the community and he thumbed his nose at us. I'm on the I Heart Eastwood committee. We're trying to make the community more attractive to businesses and families, and I have that thing living next door to me? I swear, if you planted flowers he'd piss all over them."

"Sounds infuriating."

"It was," she said.

"Infuriating enough that you'd — murder him?"

She cocked her head to one side and gave him a look like, "Seriously?"

"Is there anything else you can tell me about that night?"

"Just what I told the officer."

"What was that?"

She took an exhausted breath.

"That Kenny and his friends were up late drinking and listening to music. I went to bed and didn't see anything else."

She was growing tired of the conversation and the energy shifted to a tone where she was ready for him to leave.

"You don't know anything else about the car? Where it might be? Did anyone else drive it?"

"I really don't think so," she said, scrunching her nose. "Are we about done here?"

"One last question," he said.

"What is it?"

Logan tried to think of something.

"Nothing?"

Logan slapped his notepad against the palm of his hand. Talia stood up and ushered him out the door and followed him down the hall.

"Good luck on your case," she said, leaning back on the reception desk. Her receptionist looked up at her. "Do you have any other leads?"

"I have some things I'm following up on. If I have any more questions, is it alright if I call you?"

"The convention is coming up soon. I'm pretty busy but I've got a close eye on my phone," she said. "You dig, daddy-o?"

Logan paused to look at her face. She didn't flinch.

"I hope you find the car," she said.

The receptionist looked down at the floor.

"I'm concentrating on the Corvette right now," said Logan. "I'm hoping it's the key to finding the guy who did this."

"Hopefully your gamble pays off," said Talia. The receptionist held back a laugh, and it turned into a snort in her nose. "Are you parked outside here?"

"No," said Logan. They stood there looking at him.

"Call me if you think of anything else," he said.

"You bet I will," she said.

The receptionist ducked under the desk to keep from laughing. Logan gave them a curious look, then turned around and left.

11

Logan took the tow truck to the edge of town and turned onto the service road at the Gas n' Go on the side of the highway.

Down the road he came to a long chain link fence with weeds growing up the sides. A large weathered sign towered over the lot that said 'Rusty's RV Park and Campground' with black paint striped over an old phone number that no longer applied. A faded cartoon cowboy with chubby cheeks and a ten gallon hat waved at the traffic from the top corner of the sign.

Broken appliances and bike parts drifted against the fence as though the wind blew them there.

Logan came to the entrance and turned the corner to a gravel path that opened up to an unkempt field of mostly empty parking spaces. A few camper vans and Winnebegos laid low in their own spaces. A mongrel dog lifted its leg and peed on a truck bed camper that sat by itself in the tall grass.

Patches of trees separated a few of the lots and a couple acres away a grove of trees surrounded by farmland served as a campground.

Logan continued along the gravel road until he found a large vac truck and parked in an RV lot across from it. He climbed out of the tow truck and walked by the vac truck. It smelled like shit. An old school bus parked next to it with curtains drawn in all the windows. Piles of plastic shopping bags and the end of a mattress filled the back window.

Black garbage bags darkened the front door of the bus. Logan was about to knock when the door swung open. A man stomped down the steps holding a cooking pot and a barbecue lighter. He wore large rubber boots over pajama pants emblazoned with a pattern of the Pittsburgh Steelers logo. He wore an orange winter vest over an argyle sweater. A mesh-back baseball cap on his head showed a cartoon of a couple having sex in bed but the punchline had peeled off. The only remaining letters in the speech bubble were W and A.

He wore a thick grey moustache and his chin showed several days worth of stubble.

"I'm looking for Dennis," said Logan.

He took a moment to look Logan up and down before responding.

"You found him," he said, and turned toward a fire pit next to the bus.

"I suppose you're here about Kenny," said Dennis. "It's a damn shame. A damn shame."

He crumpled some flyers and placed kindling over top in the fire pit and lit it with the barbecue lighter.

"Did you know him well?" asked Logan.

He thought about the question as he blew on the embers and raised his eyebrows at whatever he was thinking about.

"Well enough, I suppose," he said. "We liked each other alright. I guess I was more than just an employee but I wouldn't say we were friends. We were kind of friends. Not best friends. He seemed to like me alright. I thought he was a good man."

The first licks of flame flickered around the papers and Dennis shook his head at whatever memories came to mind.

"One important thing I'm not sure you can help with," said Logan. "He had a blue Corvette Stingray."

Dennis' eyes lit up at mention of the Corvette.

"Now that was a nice car," said Dennis. "Damn fine automobile."

"You don't know where it is, do you?"

Dennis thought long and hard about the question. He looked at the fire as he prodded it with a stick. The orange light glowed against his face and sparks sailed up into the sky. He then bowed his head downward and closed his eyes in concentration. Finally, he looked back up at Logan.

"Is it at Kenny's place?"

"No, it's not," said Logan. "I was hoping you might know where it is."

Dennis thought long and hard again. Eventually he gave up, shaking his head.

"No," he said. "Can't say I do."

"That's alright," said Logan. "Did you hang out with Kenny much? Outside of work?"

"He would take me out for drinks some nights. Or sometimes we'd drink at his place and we'd watch the game. He never let me pay for nothing either. He was real good-hearted like that. Smart businessman too."

"Did he have any enemies that you know of? Anybody that would want to hurt him?"

Dennis thought good and hard about that one too and his mouth formed into a frown.

"Nobody," said Dennis. "Everybody liked Kenny. He was so funny. He shoulda been a comedian."

His gaze wandered off and he chuckled to himself when a memory arose.

"Like we were getting new tires for the truck this one time," said Dennis. "There was a young girl behind the counter. Kenny started talking like he had Downs Syndrome. He was all like, 'Mer mer mer mer mer.' And the girl was trying to be polite while she couldn't understand him. So Kenny pretends he's getting angrier and angrier and he's yelling at her in that handicapped voice, 'Mer mer mer mer mer.' And tears start welling up in her eyes because she's about to cry."

He laughed until he started coughing and then caught his breath.

"Stuff like that," he said. "Super funny guy."

"That's what people keep telling me," said Logan.

"On Halloween he had the most popular house in the neighbourhood because he gave out the extra-large size chocolate bars, cans of pop, bags of chips. He loved spoiling those kids and they'd all crowd around his door. He'd dress like Jason from the Friday the 13th movies, with the hockey mask, and jump out with a chainsaw and scare them and they'd all scream and run away."

"He sounds like a real character."

Dennis laughed some more and erupted into heavier laughter at another memory. Tears welled up in his eyes.

"One time the government census taker came to his door," Dennis had to catch his breath. He could barely get the words out. "This lady comes to the door and she said, 'Sir, I'm a government census worker and we are asking a few quick questions about the members of your household.'" Dennis caught his breath from laughing again.

"Kenny grabbed his dick and said, 'Lady, the government can suck on this member right here.'"

Dennis laughed heartily. His laughter made Logan laugh too.

"The lady ran away so fast," said Dennis, wheezing from the laughter. "But that's the way he was, you know? He was so light-hearted. Everybody loved him."

The fire lashed higher through the grill and once Dennis decided it was sufficiently hot, he unwrapped a steak from a plastic grocery bag and slapped it on the grill. He clasped a can opener to the edge of a can of beans and wound it around rim, and dumped the contents into the pot.

"Sorry, I wasn't expecting no company. Grab yourself a beer though. Grab me one while you're at it."

He nodded at the case of Gold Star leaning by the bus' back tire. Logan thanked him and grabbed them a couple beers. Dennis kicked one of the lawn chairs toward Logan and told him to have a seat.

The sun began to set and the cowboy hat of Rusty's RV Park sign silhouetted against a purple sky. The orange of the fire grew more vivid in the diminishing light.

"Don't suppose Kenny mentioned having problems with anyone?" asked Logan.

Dennis shook his head.

"Was business going OK for Kenny?" Logan asked.

"Fine," said Dennis. "He was a good businessman. We do all the properties between here and the Quaker Acres. We do the reserve. And the vacation properties around Mosquito Lake in the summer time. I went today and did the properties over past the slough there."

His face went white and he looked up at Logan with fear in his face.

"That's not illegal is it? I mean, it's Kenny's truck I guess technically. But those people were expecting me to empty their septic tanks. I'm getting the paperwork all sorted out. Or I'm going to. Just those people are expecting me. That's not illegal is it?"

"I think you're alright," said Logan.

"I mean, people are going to keep shittin'. It's gotta go somewhere."

He pronged the edge of the steak with a fork and flipped it over on the grill.

"How'd you meet Kenny?"

Dennis' eyes glazed over.

"Guess it was a long time ago now," he said, stirring the beans around in the pot. "You don't really notice the years go by, do you?"

He pressed the fork against the steak to braze it against the grill. Fat dripped down and the flames lashed higher. Logan watched his mind recall distant memories and didn't interrupt.

Dennis picked up the steak and dropped it onto a plastic camping plate on his lap, then poured the beans next to it. He cut off a piece and chewed it while his eyes looked upward.

"I was squatting in Alaska on a forestry holding," he said, a lump of steak in his cheek. "Like, land where they harvest the trees? Except they weren't doing nothing with it at the time. There was an old Indian cave there. It even had the markings on the walls, you know? Anyway, I slept in there. Trapped rabbits and foxes. Sold the fur. Sometimes I got work doing clean-up after construction jobs."

He spaced out for a moment and said, "God, I miss it. I'm too old to do that now though. But, boy I tell you, if I still had a young body like yours I'd do it again in a second.

"Well in town, they was having this big tourism push. Lots of advertising trying to get more tourists in. Everybody had to be respectful."

He said 'respectful' in a mocking tone like it was a word he was sick of hearing.

"But they really cleaned the place up. They put up a new signs on the way into town with a big picture of this big old grizzly bear out there named Buttons. Buttons the Bear was a big part of their marketing, telling people to not feed the wildlife and secure their garbage and whatnot. But also all the kids bought little stuffed teddy bears of Buttons, restaurants had Buttons-themed specials, and everybody went out on tours to try and see Buttons. Stuff like that.

"Anyway, there was this one guy. What was his name? Shit. Doesn't matter. Anyway, this guy was a trucker but he was sick of trucking. Hated it.

"And somehow or another, he figures out that some people think it's good luck to get pregnant under the Northern Lights. Like, your child will be luckier and more successful if you do that.

"He had an acreage out there and so he built some teepees on it. Filled them with furs and blankets. And he starts charging couples two hundred dollars a night to come fuck on his acreage under the Northern Lights. People came from all over. California, England, Japan. Soon enough, he's booked solid. Well, you can do the math. Making sixteen hundred dollars a night. He didn't get rich-rich, but he did better than he did trucking, that's for sure, and he didn't have to do hardly anything.

"So, the coyotes would howl at night and these tourist folks would get really scared. He'd have to convince them that everything was alright. And he had his Remington Three Seventy Five, and he'd show it to them and give them a thumbs up and strut around like John Wayne. And they thought that was pretty cool. They would clap and cheer when they saw him carrying the gun around.

"Well, sure as shit, one night Buttons the bear came around sniffing at the teepees. Real aggressive. He tried throwing rocks and hollering at it but that just pissed Buttons off more and he got more aggressive. Stood up and showed his claws and teeth like he was going to charge at him. And so he shot Buttons.

"And he had to bury it. He didn't have no hunting license and they're endangered or whatever, and it was Buttons, you know? There was going to be hell to pay for killing Buttons. He got scared, and he wanted to keep going with his teepee business. He was definitely going to get in a lot of trouble, including getting his business shut down for sure. Anyway, he drove out to my cave that night and said he'd pay me two hundred dollars to come over and help bury Buttons.

"Well, fuck. That ground was so frozen it should've been four hundred dollars but whatever. He drove me back to his place and Kenny was a buddy of his and he was there. That's where I met Kenny. Me and Kenny was up all night digging in the dark to bury this damn bear. We had to roll it into the pit, and let me tell you, that wasn't easy.

"It was almost lunch time when we finally had that bear underground. Luckily none of the tourists were up yet though because they had been up all night ... you know."

He made a circle out of his thumb and index finger on his left hand and poked the index finger of his right hand through it.

"Course you would think they would have heard the gun blast or something. But if any of them saw or heard anything, nobody said nothing. They was all happy campers the next day. Or if someone saw something, maybe they thought it was normal. Or it's one of those fucked up things you see in the middle of the night and you think 'Well, that's fucked up' and your brain files it away as a kind of nighttime apparition and you carry on with your life.

"So that guy paid us and took us out for breakfast at Trapper's Inn and basically told us to shut up about it. And that's where I met Kenny."

Dennis and Logan both took swigs from their beer cans at the same time. Dennis slurped up some beans.

"Thing is, he wasn't the same after that," he said. "People think you can just kill something and it's just one thing removed from this world and that's that. But that's not how it works. Death leaves things behind everyone has to reckon with. It follows you. Don't matter if it's a human or it's a bear. First, you get paranoid about it. Spend all your time looking over your shoulder. Plus we didn't do such a good job about burying it. I mean, hell, the ground was frozen. But he thought the government was going to show up and then he'd be done for. So he was stressing about that and he put more dirt on there. Then he got all kind of insects and crows and coyotes coming around as the body decomposed. The critters started disrupting his business. It wasn't so much paradise anymore.

"So he was up all night trying to scare these things away. He got less and less sleep and started acting funny. The feel wasn't the same out there and he got fewer people to come stay out at his place.

"He got really religious or philosophical about it. He thought the bear was this spiritual thing sent by God and he had killed it and so it was only matter of time before his crime against God caught up to him. And the fact that less tourists were coming to his place was God's punishment against him. Of course it was just him being crazy, but that's what killing does to you. You get a little crazy.

"Anyway, that's where I met Kenny but that was a long time ago. And it was just about four years ago we ran into each other again here in town. I was at the grocery store and he saw me and he took me to the peelers in the middle of the afternoon. And he said he needed someone to drive his sump truck and that was it."

The fire hissed as Dennis scraped the scraps off his plate and then rinsed his plate off under a four gallon jug of water perched on the hood of the bus. The sky flooded with a gritty tangerine orange, a shade you only get in Edmonton when the sun moves off its summertime axis and rolls south of the city each day and creates long shadows throughout the day. Logan finished his beer and made small talk. The dusky orange gave way to shades of purple and gold drifting into the sky behind Dennis. Tree branches and the shape of Rusty's cowboy hat on the big sign silhouetted black against the sky. Logan and Dennis sat there a while, watching the fire as the sun went down without the need for either of them to say anything.

Logan's phone rang. The ringtone was a brash Latin pop song put on there by the phone's owner. It jarred them both from the state they settled into while looking at the fire. It was Ricky calling.

"Hey, what's going on?" asked Ricky.

"I'm at Rusty's RV Park," said Logan.

"Did you find the car?"

"Nah," said Logan.

"There's been another murder," said Ricky.

"What do you mean?"

"A woman shot on her couch and she had a QR code on the wall above her head, just like Kenny," said Ricky.

"Where was it?"

"The news article said 88th Street and 124th Ave. I'll do some digging. So should you."

"Alright."

"Alright."

12

Logan parked the tow truck by a long sound barrier wall that shielded the densely packed neighbourhood from the traffic noise of the Yellowhead Highway on the other side.

Little homes huddled next to each other and slowly let themselves crumble. Some were patched up with makeshift repairs — a deck propped up on cinder blocks, a tarp tied down over a garage roof, a picture of Jesus Christ nailed over the hole above a door where a porch light was removed.

The news article didn't give the exact address of the murder victim's house, only that her house situated itself somewhere on the block of 88th Street and 124th Ave but before long he came across a house with a single streamer of yellow police tape slung between a tree on the lawn across to the neighbour's fence on the other side. Flags emblazoned with the heavy metal band Slipknot covered the basement windows and the lights were off inside. Logan strolled around back.

In the back alley, an old orange camper van slumped down next to the back fence and didn't look as though it had much intention of going anywhere. The back windows were as dark as the front. Wood pallets stacked against each other near a fire pit in the middle of the backyard.

Logan walked the length of the back alley. Neighbours put up signs like 'Beware of dog' and 'Smile you're on camera'. One house showed a picture of a shotgun with the words 'We don't call 911'.

Logan rounded the corner back toward the front of the house when he heard a vehicle slowly rolling behind him. Logan stopped walking and grimaced up at the sky.

A 'WHOOP WHOOP' bleeted out from behind him. Logan turned around as Detective Darius Days' burgundy SUV pulled up next to him.

"What a coincidence," said Days. "Imagine running into you here."

"How's it going?" asked Logan.

"Get in," said Days.

Logan climbed in the back seat. Days pulled the SUV over to the curb at the end of the block.

"What did I say about finding you at my crime scene?" asked Days.

"Technically we were talking about a different crime scene," said Logan. "This is a whole other crime scene."

Detective Days looked him in the eyes with an unamused expression on his face.

"You going to tell me what happened here?"

"You know more than I do," said Logan. "All I know is what was in the news."

"What are you doing here?"

"Looking for the Corvette."

"What makes you think the Corvette would be around here?"

"The details in the news gave my boss Ricky a vibe," said Logan. "He told me to look around."

"Does Ricky get a lot of vibes?"

"I suppose he does," said Logan. "He's pretty intuitive."

"Is that so?"

Days let a silence hang in the air and kept staring at Logan. Logan stared back, opening his eyes wide mockingly.

"Is anybody in there?" asked Logan.

"The victim's boyfriend is in there, wiping blood and brains off the wall," said Days.

"What's his name?"

"I couldn't say."

"Like you don't know or you won't tell me?" asked Logan.

"I won't tell you."

"Why not?"

"It doesn't behoove me," said Days.

"Is he a suspect?"

"Everybody's a suspect," said Days. "What have you figured out about this Corvette?"

"Nothing, honestly," said Logan. "That's why I'm here. I was hoping to get lucky."

Days mulled it over. He opened his mouth as though he were about to ask another question but seemed to change his mind.

"You can go," he said. "Don't let me catch you knocking on that door. He's been through enough."

Logan got out of the SUV and took one more long look at the little house with the darkened windows and then made his way back to the tow truck and drove it back to the shop.

Clare's white Toyota Camry pulled up in front of Logan's apartment building, the front tire rolling up onto the curb, and thumping back down onto the street in a way that made Logan close one eye and grunt.

Logan got in the passenger seat and neither said much right away but after a few seconds Clare made small talk about the radio, the weather, and the rising price of whatever. Gas or beef or commodities or something.

She pulled into the lot behind a cafe near the university and they entered.

Fresh baking smells floated over from the kitchen in the back and the clamor of various conversations filled the room. Logan ordered a black coffee. Clare ordered a chai latte and stirred it with a cinnamon stick.

"We had to put Hugo down," she said.

"Damn. I'm sorry," said Logan.

"It's OK," she said. "He was in a lot of pain and it wasn't going to get any better."

"Are you OK?"

"I'll be fine," she said, making eye contact. "Toward the end he just curled up under the step, like he didn't want to be a burden."

"I think it's probably a survival instinct thing," said Logan. "A lot of animals will hide when they're sick to keep predators away from the pack."

"Yeah," she said. "Something like that."

She sipped her latte.

"We held a service for him. Just the two of us. Ricky wore a tie."

"Get the hell out of town," said Logan. "I don't believe you for a second."

"Honest to God," she said. "Ricky wore a tie, and we lit some candles. We said a prayer. We looked at photos from when Hugo was just a puppy. Here, look at this."

She held up her phone and flipped through a few photos of the little bulldog sitting at the dinner table with a party hat on his head. Strips of sirloin sat in front of him with a birthday candle sticking out. Hugo glowered with an air of entitlement.

"He looks like he wished you'd stop wasting his time with party hats and photographs."

Clare gave a little laugh.

"Hugo always had big plans for the day. Chewing and farting, mostly, and he did not like to be interrupted."

Logan passed her phone back to her.

"Then Ricky took him to the dump and we went out for dinner," she said and took a deep breath.

"It must be quiet around there," said Logan.

"There's less slobber everywhere, that's for sure," she said. "We'll get another one soon. Not a bulldog though. Something else. Ricky wants a boxer but those dogs are so insane. I don't know how anyone could sleep with those things. I want a corgi. I don't know. We'll see."

"Trixie and Dixie not enough dogs for Rickie?"

"Those are junkyard dogs," she said with a playful 'obviously' ring in her voice. "We need a little buddy for around the house."

She turned her coffee cup clockwise in front of her while she pondered how to approach the next part of the conversation. Logan leaned back and waited.

"How are you doing, Logan?"

"I'm fine," he said.

"Are you really?" she said. "Is there anything you want to talk about? How are you feeling?"

She was playing therapist again. Getting Logan to talk about his feelings as an entry point to what a bag of shit he is.

"I can't think of anything," he said.

"How's work?"

"Work's work."

"Are you looking for other jobs?"

"I was," said Logan. "Had some interviews. By the time I get to the them they've already made their mind up they don't want me."

"I'm sure there's more to it than that," she said, but then forced a little smile to let him know she wasn't going to wring the issue out much further.

"I'll get back at it," said Logan.

"I just worry about you is all," she said.

"I'm fine."

"Are you though? You don't look fine."

"I'm getting some cars for Ricky," said Logan. "Things are fine."

"I don't think spending all that money at the casino was the best choice," she said.

"I was about to quadruple my money but a Russian was cheating and the staff at that casino can't do their jobs right."

"There's always going to be cheaters," she said. "Life is always going to be like that. I don't like seeing you like this."

"Like what? I'm fine," he said.

"But when are you —" she started before catching herself. She pushed her lips out and then sucked them into her mouth and slowly released them. In a calmer voice she said, "What do you want for yourself? Don't you want anything? Don't you want to do anything with your life? Travel? Anything?"

"I'm fine," he said, and it may have been one too many 'fines' because her face flushed hot and red.

"You're not fine," she said. "You live in that little apartment with nothing. It honestly looks like you're squatting. Do you even have a TV yet?"

"I don't like TV."

She closed her eyes and shook her head.

"You're being difficult," she said.

"Do I have to like TV?"

"It's weird to not have a TV," she said.

"If you say so."

She shut her eyes tight and swallowed.

"It's just," she started, and a lump caught in her throat. "This is the first time I've ever had anything resembling normal. Or nice. It will never be perfectly normal but it's pretty close and I need you to be OK too."

"I'm fi—" he began, but she glared at him before he could finish the word.

"It would be nice if you could get your shit together," she said, the words finally spilling out of her mouth.

"Sorry, I don't have Ricky taking care of me," he said.

"You do have Ricky taking care of you," she shot back. "He has done nothing but give you opportunities and jobs when no one else would."

"He's a loan shark," Logan snapped back. "Everything he's ever done for me is to keep me under his thumb."

"Oh get a load of yourself," she said. "You really are unbelievable, you know that? Everything was awful until we met Ricky. How can you be so ungrateful?"

"I should be grateful Ricky's the boss of me," said Logan. "Got it."

Clare unrolled a cloth napkin from around a knife and fork and wiped her mouth with it. Once she did, she threw it down on the table and massaged an eyebrow with the side of her hand.

"We just care about you is all," she said, squaring herself in her seat and folding the napkin, carefully making the edges meet. Emotions still bubbled under the surface and she avoided eye contact with Logan to keep from crying.

"Hey," said Logan. "I'm sorry I'm an asshole. I'm working on it."

That helped some.

"I'm working on the Corvette," said Logan. "Ricky said you want to go to school."

"Interior Design," she said. "I think I'd be good at it."

"I think you'll be great at it," said Logan. "You've got a good eye."

"I've been drawing a lot," she said.

"Really? I'd love to see some."

"Absolutely not," she said, her mood lifting. "They're bad."

She chuckled a bit.

"The Corvette would be a huge relief as far as that goes."

"Ricky seems like he has money," Logan said, more as a question.

"Sort of," she said. "Not much liquidity though. All his money is tied up in things. And he keeps those things in other people's names. My name, a lot of the time. He says it's so if those lawyer jackals ever come for him then there's not much meat on the bone."

Logan nodded.

They finished their drinks and she asked if he needed a ride anywhere. Logan said he'd give her directions to Delton so he could talk to someone about the Corvette. They got in her Camry and they made their way out of the trendy restaurant district near the university through downtown and back across the river.

"Once you're an interior designer are you going to re-do that house?" asked Logan.

"We've already started," she said. "Little things. You get to living in a place so long and after a while it becomes a blender of old things. A jumbled mess. So we're starting to talk about what our style is. How we want to live. I consider it a form of self-care. It's important."

The traffic on the bridge was a bit backed up but surged forward in gradual waves.

"We're just doing little things right now. The lights. Rugs. That kind of thing," she continued. "Down the road we have big plans though. Ricky wants to move his office to where my bedroom is now."

The sun blinked off and on over Logan's eyes between the steel beams as they drove along the Stafford Bridge.

"Know what we're thinking?" she said. "We could build my own bedroom apartment for me up in the trees behind the house. Can you imagine? A luxurious bedroom treehouse?"

Logan pointed out the turns to take them back to the crime scene in Delton.

They pulled up to the rundown little house on 88th Street and 124th Avenue with Slipknot flags in the windows. The yellow police tape was still tied across the lawn but had twisted and sagged to the ground.

"Cute," said Clare.

"There's a fixer-upper for you," said Logan as he stepped out of the vehicle.

"Hey," Clare called after him before he closed the door. She leaned over the console to look out at him through the passenger door.

"Thank you," she said.

"What for?"

"For trying."

He nodded and closed the door. He surveyed the street for Detective Days' SUV or any other police vehicles but didn't see any, so he walked up to the steps to the front door and rang the doorbell and rapped his knuckle on the flyscreen.

There was some rummaging around inside. A shuffling of items. Then a man wearing camouflage cargo pants and a t-shirt branded with auto racing performance oil opened the door. A pair of aviator sunglasses settled above an orange beard. He leaned against the door frame while he waited for Logan to speak.

"Sorry to bother you," said Logan and then struggled to find the words to say next.

"Yup," said they guy who then walked away leaving the door open behind him and waved for Logan to follow. "Just about everyone and their dog has come around to ask questions. Might as well come on in."

Logan looked back and Clare drove away. He entered. The house reeked of cannabis and cleaning chemicals. He turned the corner and saw a faded but ruddy shade of brown smeared all over the far wall in circular motions above a couch. A blanket covered the couch.

"If you're the owner of the house, then you have to clean your wife's brains and blood off the wall," said the guy. "The city don't help you or nothing. They'll refer you to a session with a psychiatrist at a community clinic but they won't help clean up your wife's brains off the wall. Isn't that fucked up?"

His body plodded around in a slow, lumbering pace. Signs of distress showed in pained, sharp lines in his forehead and around his eyes, all pointing to the centre of his face.

"You want a beer?" he asked.

13

The man in the camouflage pants and racing oil t-shirt shuffled over to the fridge. Logan turned his head away from the blood-smeared living room wall.

"I mean, we weren't married-married," said the guy. "We were engaged. You want a beer?"

Logan declined. The guy cracked open a beer and kicked the fridge door closed. Logan hovered near the blanket-covered couch. The guy waved his hand gesturing for Logan to sit. Logan sat on the edge of the couch.

Dishes piled up on the counters. Cardboard boxes stacked up on the dining table and spread back in piles all the way to the far wall of the dining room. A plastic bong lay on its side on the living room floor next to the coffee table. A bucket full of soapy dark water and a bloody rag rested on top of the coffee table. Clifford picked it up and moved it to the washroom and Logan listened to him pour it into the bathtub.

Clifford returned and flopped down in a worn out recliner with burn holes on the the armrests and well-worn groove in the middle that fit the shape of his body.

He flicked on the TV. One of those shows where people travel to diners across the country to eat over-sized helpings of heart attack food blinked on the screen. He kept the volume low so it was only a murmur in the background. Then he leaned forward and pulled a plastic container from the coffee table closer to himself. He pulled out some pot and pinched some into a rolling paper.

"These shows are all fuckin' fake," he said. His eyes swam around somewhat intoxicated. Logan craned his neck, trying to make eye contact.

"They're pretty ridiculous," said Logan.

The man inspected Logan out the side of his eye as he licked the joint and sealed it.

"Cliff," he said, extending his hand.

"Logan." They shook hands.

"What do you want to know?" asked Cliff.

"What happened?" asked Logan.

Cliff lit his joint and puffed on it. Once it burned consistently, he held it up toward Logan. Logan declined with a wave of his hand.

"Me and a buddy were mowing some lawns," said Clifford. He spoke with his nose plugged as he held in the smoke. He turned the joint in his mouth as he puffed on it. "Then by the time we had the mowers and trimmers locked up, and I drove my friend home, it must have been six or six-thirty. The back door was still locked and there were no signs of forced entry, eh? So he must have come in through the front door. She was on the couch."

A lightning bolt-shaped vein bulged out the centre of his forward and pain flashed across his eyes. It took him a moment to bury the emotions.

Logan didn't say anything and let Clifford collect himself.

"He shot her right there, man. A bunch of times. And I came home and found her there. She was all laid out —"

Clifford pointed to where Logan was sitting and cried more audibly this time, a thick, choking sob bubbled out of his throat and he threw his head forward between his knees.

Logan leaned forward to stand up but then changed his mind.

Clifford stood up again and paced around the living room, into the kitchen and back, crying and puffing on his joint. He growled occasionally, as though something gnawed at his insides.

"I can't do this," he said. "I'm not OK."

"It's going to be OK," said Logan. "What was her name?"

Cliff paced a bit more.

"Brooke. Brooke Esterly."

He wiped his forehead and rubbed his eyes and flopped back down in the cigarette burned recliner.

"I served in Afghanistan, hey?" he said, the creases around his eyes pointing more deeply at the centre of his face.

"I can't imagine," said Logan. "I respect the hell out of that."

Cliff clutched his middle and closed his eyes like he was going to explode.

"You want so much to leave it over there and it follows you here," he said. He leaned forward and rested his head in his hands.

Logan waited. Cliff mumbled to himself.

"Summertime — and all the heat — crawling —"

"Question for you," said Logan, loudly. Cliff put himself back together. "Was there a blue Corvette Stingray around that day or any day? You see any blue Corvettes around?"

He found a picture of one on his phone and showed it to Cliff.

"Holy shit," said Cliff. "Yeah, I saw that car around. It was parked in front of our house a couple times and up the block. Is that the guy who did this?"

"I'm not sure," said Logan. "If we can find that car, I think it might tell us a lot."

"Yeah, we got to find him, man," said Cliff.

"Did you see the driver?"

"Kind of. I don't remember much. He was wearing sunglasses. I think he was white. There was glare on the windshield and I wasn't really paying attention.

"Is it possible Brooke knew them?"

"I really don't think so," said Cliff. "We don't know anybody with a Corvette. We don't get out all that much."

Logan looked over his shoulder at the wall behind him and saw some scrapes in the drywall amongst the brown smears above his head.

"Was there a sticker or anything on the wall when you saw her? A QR code or something?" asked Logan.

Cliff squinted his eyes.

"You don't seem like a cop," he said. "Why are you here?"

"I'm a private investigator working a separate case that I think is related to this one."

Cliff thought about it and found it acceptable enough.

"Yeah, like the bar code? It was right above her. The cops used my dish soap and putty knife to scrape it off the wall and took it as evidence. It was about that big." He formed a square with his fingers. "They couldn't tell me anything about it. They said because it's still an active investigation but I don't think they know shit. Plus I'm a suspect."

The lightning bolt vein flashed on his face along with the creases around his eyes. The pain sprung upon him without warning and he would bury it within himself again by forcing a docile expression on his face.

"Who do you think did this?" asked Logan.

Clifford took a long drag of his joint and leaned back as he exhaled. He offered the joint again. Logan waved his hand.

"Shit, man. I don't know. Brooke was such a sweet person. No one would want to hurt her. She kept to herself. She didn't even know hardly anyone. She spent most of her time playing Shadow Realm 3. You played that? It's a pretty messed up game. She was really good at it. She made bracelets and necklaces and sold them out of the Salvation Army thrift store. It wasn't much but it made her happy. You know what I mean? Like, that was it. She didn't do nothing else."

Logan let it rest. They both turned to the TV. On the screen, the hosts were in an Alaskan diner eating a cheeseburger the size of a football. Meat and cheese spilled out the sides like a volcanic eruption and they lifted the burgers above their faces to catch the dripping mess in their mouths.

"Did she have any friends?"

"Not a lot," said the guy. "Her old friends from high school, kind of. But they were all scrubs that only used her. I managed to convince her for the most part they were no good for her. Every once in a while they'd come through town and they'd party. It would always end up in fighting and tears. So she saw them less and less."

"Would any of them want to hurt her?"

The guy responded with a hiss as he pinched off the lit end of the joint and placed the remainder in a marble ash tray next to the recliner.

"Those idiots like to fight and argue but it's only for the drama," he said. "They can't hold a grudge past the next weekend. None of them are capable of something like this. When they hear Brooke's gone it will only be something for them to be dramatic about for a couple weeks, and then they'll move on to something else."

He pulled a pack of cigarettes out of his pocket and put one in his mouth.

Clifford's eyes grew bleary. He puffed and blew the smoke up toward the ceiling.

Logan watched the television screen where the restaurant made a plate with the hosts' faces and put it on the wall. It was a moment before he realized Clifford had his head down, sobbing quietly.

"It's gonna be OK, man," said Logan.

"Do you think I'm a suspect?"

"They have to suspect everyone around her as part of the process. They'll take a look at it and see you're fine. It'll be OK."

"There's no way I can go to jail," said Cliff. "I'm barely hanging on."

Cliff closed his eyes and disappeared inside himself.

"You mind hanging out for a bit?" he said, opening his eyes again. "I have pot. Beer."

"I can hang out for a bit," said Logan. "I don't mind. Why don't you tell me how you and Brooke met?"

Cliff's head sunk down into his chest again and he got quiet.

"Sorry. If you don't want to talk about it we can talk about something else."

"No, I don't mind," said Cliff. "We met at the downtown Denny's in the middle of the night one night. Her friends were out partying and my buddy knew some of them, and everybody met up at Denny's after the bars closed. We hit it off and got to talking. We got to flirting over text until one day she asked if I wanted to come over and I did. She didn't really like being home alone. She was scared of being home invaded. So she called me over more and more until eventually I just never left."

Something pained him deep inside for a moment. Then a funny memory struck him and he laughed.

"We were all playing a game in the diner that first night. Everyone was a little drunk. We took turns saying the name of an animal in the spirit of that animal."

He laughed harder.

"Mon-KEY," he said, in a screechy voice.

He laughed. Logan stared at him. He turned and looked Logan dead in the eye.

"Thnake," he said, and laughed some more. Logan let out a chuckle.

"Crow," he cawed, and closed his eyes and curled up in the recliner, unable to control his laughter. "You do one."

"I'm good," said Logan.

"No, you have to," he said.

"Cow," said Logan, in a low deadpan.

Cliff's face went red with laughter.

"More, more," he said.

"Whale," said Logan, in a similar low, droopy voice. He made his Adam's apple drop in his throat to imitate a whale's sonar.

Cliff held his stomach as he laughed and the laugh turned into a fit of coughing. Out of breath, he spun his finger in a wheel motion in the air to ask for more.

"COCK," yelled Logan in a loud cowboy accent.

Cliff laughed so hard he kicked out the footrest and the recliner fell backwards. He landed on his back still laughing and wriggled off the chair so he was flat on the floor.

"I'm sorry," said Logan.

Cliff shook his head and laughed some more.

"Lie down here," said Cliff. "Laugh with me."

"What?"

"Laugh with me. It's good for you."

"I should get going, man," said Logan. "Maybe I should get your number. In case you see the Corvette."

"Lie down."

Logan laid down on the ground with his head next to Cliff's. Their bodies pointed in opposite directions. Logan's feet pointed north toward the door. Cliff's feet pointed south. They both looked up at the ceiling.

"S-s-s-lothhhh," said Cliff, unable to contain his joy. Then he got deadly serious.

There was quiet a moment. He turned his head to face Logan.

"Octoputh," he said, like a big dummy and buckled with laughter.

"What's your phone number, man?" asked Logan. "I got to go."

"One more," said Cliff. "Do one more."

Logan folded his hands on his chest.

"Orangutan," said Logan, like a wise old wizard.

Clifford's back arched as he laughed.

"Tarantula," said Cliff, like a vampire.

Logan bleated out an elephant noise with his lips and failed at making it blend into the word 'elephant'.

Cliff looked over at him until he had Logan's attention. Logan looked over.

With a debonair smile Cliff said, "Crocodile."

They traded animals back and forth in funny voices.

"Penguin."

"Buffalo."

"Hyena."

"Mosquito."

"Llama."

"Ostrich."

Cliff stopped laughing. He closed his eyes.

"Hey," said Logan, sitting up. "Give me your number and put mine in your phone."

Cliff mumbled out his number. Logan stood up and tapped the number into his phone and told him his number. Cliff texted him.

"Yo, it's Cliff," it read.

"Moose," said Cliff.

"OK, man, take care," said Logan standing up. "I got to go but I'll call you later."

Logan stepped over to the doorway and looked back at Cliff. He was already asleep on the floor.

Logan awoke to the blaring Latin pop song bursting out of the phone on the floor next to his bed.

He looked at the time. It was the middle of the night.

"Hello?"

"Hey. It's Cliff."

"Cliff, what's going on, man?"

Logan rubbed his eyes with his thumb and forefinger.

"You think that Corvette is pretty important, hey?"

"Yeah, I do."

"We should go look for it."

"That's kind of what I've been doing."

"Let's go look for it right now."

"It's the middle of the night."

"What are you doing right now?"

"Sleeping."

"Well let's go. I'm going to find it. I know I can find it right now."

"Can't we do this tomorrow?"

"Why?"

"I kind of have stuff to do. Work, and stuff."

Cliff's breath rattled through the phone speaker, wet and close to the microphone.

"Come on," said Cliff.

"What?"

"Come on," he said again.

"What?"

"What do you do for a living?"

"What do you mean?" said Logan.

"You're not an investigator."

"Uh, yeah I am." Logan tried to find the words. "Pretty much. I'm a Collateral Acquisitions Agent."

"You're a repo man."

"More or less."

"OK, well I'm going to help you find the car, Logan," said Cliff.

"Does it have to be right now?"

"Yeah. We're going to find it tonight. I can feel it. What's your address?"

Logan gave his address and half an hour later Cliff pulled up in front of Logan's apartment building. He called again to say he had arrived and Logan grabbed his jacket and thumped his way down the steps to the street.

"Rise and shine," said Cliff as Logan got into the large pick up truck. Ladders and rakes were fastened against a wooden rack that extended up both sides of the back. Hard rock radio from "The Bear" 100.3 FM chugged away through the truck's speakers.

"Got you a coffee," said Cliff, passing over a cup. "Thanks for coming. We can find this car. I know it."

Logan peeled open the plastic tab on the coffee and smelled it first. It was sweet and creamy. He took a sip.

"Where did you want to start?"

"Northeast," said Cliff. "I figured start there and wind our way out to the other communities around it. Hit up as much as we can."

"You've been through a lot," said Logan. "This doesn't seem like the best use of our time if we want to find the Corvette."

"We can find it," Cliff shot back.

"I don't know, man."

"Please," said Cliff. His eyes glistened and the pained lines formed around the edges of his face. "We have to."

Logan sighed and then settled in his seat and waved his hand toward the road ahead.

"For a little while," said Logan. "I gotta get back though. I have things to do."

Cliff pulled out into the street and took Fort Road to the farthest edge of the city. From there they crawled along darkened streets, scrutinizing all the vehicles along the road.

"Back at my house you said there was another case like Brooke. What happened?"

Cliff was sober now, and alert. He leaned over the wide steering wheel as though he was willing the truck forward with his frontal lobe.

"A guy in town was killed. Shot. Had a QR code on the wall above where he was killed. Do you or Brooke know a guy named Kenny Prince?"

Cliff thought about it and shook his head.

"What do we know about this guy?

"He was kind of rough around the edges. Liked to party. He drove sump trucks for a living and he used to live in Alaska. Hard to surmise much else."

Cliff lifted his coffee to his lips without taking his eyes off the road and thought about Kenny and shook his head again.

"Yeah. Don't know him. What do you make of these QR codes?"

"Something cold and mechanical about them. I tried scanning one. It went to a 404 page."

"Confirming the kill," said Cliff.

"You think so?"

Cliff nodded and took another sip of coffee.

They weaved their way up one street, and down another, back and forth. Almost all the vehicles they passed were ten-year old SUVs and four door sedans in conservative monochrome tones or faded pastel colours.

"They don't make cool cars anymore," said Cliff. "You ever notice that? They're all just these plastic egg carton go-karts. I say that because they're designed to crumple like egg cartons. No kind of engine in them. But they didn't get any cheaper. They got more expensive. Take you twenty years to pay one of them off and they don't even last twenty years anymore. What's that about?"

"I wish I knew," said Logan.

A light mist floated under street lamps. Some of the lamps emitted an orange glow into the mist, others a harsh white. The clanking of the truck down the street sounded distinct in the broad silence of the late night, and the silence they around them felt as though it stretched for miles.

They wound their way off the smaller residential streets onto a wider straight-away to the next neighbourhood.

"I'm going to find the guy who did this and I'm going to kill him," said Cliff without taking his eyes off the road, still leaning over the steering wheel. "I'm going to kill him and then disappear into the bush."

"You should probably let the justice system take care of him. You don't want to throw your life away."

Cliff didn't say anything for a moment and then said, "For sure. Then I'm going to go out to the bush. I served in Afghanistan, hey?"

Cliff looked over at Logan for the first time to gauge his reaction.

"You mentioned back at your house," said Logan. "I have a lot of respect for that."

Cliff nodded as though Logan had answered a question correctly.

"Army taught me how to live out in the wild. I can go out there. Then I'll just be free."

"But if you killed him, you'd be in hiding. So you wouldn't be totally free. In the truest sense of the word."

Cliff shot Logan an annoyed kind of look out of the side of his eye and then shrugged.

"All in how you look at it. Back in old Western days if you committed a crime, you got exiled. They'd give you a horse and a gun and they'd slap the horse on the ass and send you out of town. So that guy has to go out and live off the land. That guy's banished. Ends up foraging for himself out in the bush a few hundred yards away from a guy who chooses to live like that and likes it."

Cliff laughed to himself at the idea.

"That's me. You just have to decide you want to live by the laws of the wild instead of civilization."

They continued to watch out the window, scrutinizing the occasional car that passed by on the road.

"I like the city," said Logan. "It's wild too in its own way."

"Concrete jungle," said Cliff. "All it takes is for some foreign enemy hackers to decide to turn the lights out. That's how World War Three is going to be fought, you know. Not bombs and soldiers in trenches. It'll be hackers shutting down utilities. Can't turn the lights out on me if I'm already in the dark."

"Fair enough," said Logan. "I'll keep playing poker at the casino until that day comes though."

Cliff laughed again and sipped his coffee.

HONK! A bunch of kids packed into a four-door Kia came up right behind them and honked the horn at Cliff's truck.

Cliff swore and looked at the rear view mirror and then at the side view mirror. The car lunged toward them and honked again. Cliff sped up and the car stayed right behind them.

"Hang on," said Cliff. He slammed on the brakes and the car squealed behind them as it braked as well. The carload of kids came up beside them, swerving toward them. They rolled down their windows and gave the finger and swore at Cliff. They swerved again toward the truck and then sped off.

Cliff gunned the acceleration and raced after them. Logan clutched at the handle above the door.

They swerved across all the lanes, giving the finger out the back window.

The road came to a T-intersection in front of a pharmacy and a barbershop. The Kia went to make a right turn and that's where Cliff caught them, and rammed the back end of the Kia and sent it spinning into the far sidewalk in front of the barbershop.

"Fuck, Cliff, what are you doing?"

The truck slammed to a stop and Cliff leapt out and stomped up to the car with his fists clenched.

"Everybody out of the car now," he yelled, his eyes bulging with red intensity. "You're all fucking dead."

Logan muttered under his breath and got out of the truck. No one got out of the car. The back right side of the Kia was smashed in. The back left tire buckled underneath the car against the curb of the sidewalk.

Cliff slapped the palms of his hands on the trunk of the car.

"Let's go," he yelled. "Out!"

"Cliff. Stop."

Cliff kicked the back bumper.

"Everybody out. Now."

"Cliff."

Logan wedged his way between Cliff and the car and started pushing him backward. Cliff heaved from side to side, trying to look around Logan's head to concentrate on the kids in the car. Logan kept pushing him backward.

"Cliff, will you quit it? What are you doing?"

"Standing up for myself," said Cliff. "Teaching these kids a goddamn lesson."

"Let it go," said Logan. "You're not fixing anything."

"I'm about to fix these fucking idiots right here."

Logan pushed Cliff backward, Cliff shoved Logan, and Logan returned the shove.

"Cliff, look at me. Look at me. Hey, stop. Look at me."

Cliff looked Logan in the eyes. Eyes blazing. Shoulders reared back. Hands grappling the air at his sides.

"Look at me. Look at me. This isn't going to find whoever did this to Brooke. Alright? Don't throw your mission away on these kids. When the cops get here, then what? What have you gained?"

Cliff mulled it over and his eyes relaxed a bit and he seemed to recognize something in Logan's eyes a bit better. A kind of trust settled in his eyes.

Cliff turned away as he wrestled with his thoughts. A ghostly white pall cast over him as he passed under a street lamp with a mist hovering in the air. He charged back at the car. Then stopped himself and walked away again.

"Maybe you're right," he said.

The sound of police sirens whined in the background.

"Do you want to find Brooke's killer or not?" asked Logan. He pulled at Cliff's sleeve and Cliff reluctantly leaned back toward the truck. "Let's go."

Cliff and Logan climbed back into the truck and Cliff turned around the corner and out of the neighbourhood. Behind them, police lights streaked toward the smashed Kia.

They zig-zagged their way through the back streets, each darker and more obscure than the last to avoid any run-ins with police. A warehouse district emerged around them with fewer street lamps so the streets were darker and Cliff pulled into an unlit parking lot and turned off the engine.

"Let's just hang out here for a bit until we feel like it's safe to get back on the road."

They both listened to the night and when they didn't hear police sirens they slid down in their seats and relaxed a bit more.

"Thanks for stopping me back there," said Cliff.

"It's alright."

"I'm not thinking so straight these days. I kind of fly off the handle."

"It's all good. I just didn't want you to do something you'd regret."

"Thanks."

The silence of the night remained calm and still. Cliff opened the door and stepped out of the driver's side. He breathed in the fresh air deeply and meandered across the parking lot to the street. He looked up and down the road and didn't see anything and moseyed back across the parking lot. Logan got out of the truck and stretched.

The parking lot faced a wide, grey warehouse. Empty, apparently, with dusty doors with cobwebs in the corners. A 'For Lease' banner sagged from the top of the building. Hundreds of glass panes, each not much bigger than a beer coaster, striped across the building high up on wall below the banner. Each glass pane was apparently thick, concaved with a small circular pattern. Several spaces showed a square of darkness from where several had been smashed out. The result looked something like a randomized chess board of dark squares and squares of pallid glass reflecting the moonlight.

Logan watched Cliff look up at the night sky but when Cliff turned away Logan realized Cliff was holding back tears.

"Why does this keep happening to me?"

"What are you talking about?"

"I try to do something and everything blows up in my hands," Cliff choked out.

"You're all good," said Logan.

"It's been like this since I got back from the Middle East."

Cliff sniffed in a deep breath and controlled his emotions.

"I feel like Brooke is my fault too."

"Of course not. That had nothing to do with you."

Cliff stalked around the parking lot and thought about it. A line of street lamps separated a row of empty parking spaced down the middle of the lot and each lamp stood in a bed of small rocks. Cliff picked up a rock and flung it at the small glass panel windows and hit the wall just below them.

"If I knew what happened to Brooke, then I could at least have something to pin it on. Not knowing, it's like a dark evil energy always following me around. It's like I brought it with me from the war and it's all my fault."

"I swear to God it's not your fault," said Logan.

Cliff picked up another rock and hurled it at the window panes. He hit one and the rock bounced off.

"See that hole in the middle? Surrounded by the glass squares? You gotta get it in there."

Logan nodded and picked up a rock.

"You can't step past this line," said Cliff, tracing a yellow parking line with his toe.

Logan flung the rock and it sailed up above the windows. Cliff threw again and hit just below. Logan sent another rock in a high arc that bounced off one of the windows.

"I'll help you find this Corvette, man," said Cliff. "Can you keep me in the loop? I won't get in your way or nothing. If I have someone else's face to put this on, then I know it's not my fault. It's not some dark energy I bring around with me."

"Yeah, that's no problem," said Logan. Logan tossed another rock and it sailed bounced off a glass pane next to the dark hole. Cliff threw a rock that hit above the stripe of glass panels.

"Promise?" asked Cliff.

"For sure."

Logan flung a rock and it sailed through the dark hole in the centre. Cliff glanced over at him.

"Nice one," he said.

Cliff chucked his rock and it smashed a window pane next to the hole and the crashing glass echoed loudly across the warehouse lots.

"We should get out of here."

"Yeah."

They got back into the truck and agreed to call it a night. Cliff drove Logan home and as he pulled up outside Logan's apartment, each told the other they would call if there were any developments on finding the Stingray.

14

"Might have been a gang initiation thing," said Ricky. He propped his foot on a box of wrench sockets behind the till. Logan leaned on the counter while Tom stood at the other end and worked on untangling a wad of phone chargers and headphones.

"The QR codes are weird though," said Logan. "It's too sophisticated for street thugs and I don't see real gangsters sticking evidence to the wall."

Ricky wagged his head from side to side as he thought about it.

Tom put the tangle of wires down and walked over to the till. He grabbed a set of keys from under the coin tray and opened the metal cage around the old Coke machine at the back. Then he opened the machine itself and helped himself to a can of Coke and locked it back up again.

"Those things cost money, you know," Ricky snapped at him.

"I don't have any cash on me," said Tom, ducking his head a bit as he walked in front of Ricky to return the keys to the cash register. Ricky glared at him as he walked past.

"I swear to God people will bleed you fucking dry," Ricky muttered to himself. Tom took his can of pop and bundle of wires and made himself scarce in the back.

Ricky slapped some papers onto the counter.

"A little Roadster," said Ricky. "Signee is one mister Jax Hickey. A lawyer. He's a pathological liar. A ruthless, greedy son of a bitch. And he's cute too, so he's exactly my type. Problem is, he's defaulted on his payments to me so fuck him."

Logan scanned the papers.

"A condo," Logan groaned. "It's harder to get cars out of the underground parking."

"You'll think of something," said Ricky.

Logan went around back and got in the tow truck, turned the ignition, and it rumbled to life. It clanked and shuddered all the way down 82nd Street and around to Jasper Avenue to a cluster of condo-buildings overlooking the river valley. The front facade showed reflective gold-coloured glass while the sides of the buildings showed the old brick walls revealing they used to be low-income apartments now converted into expensive condos.

Logan parked in the 10-minute loading zone in front of the building and walked to the buzzer directory in the lobby and buzzed the number written on the contract. No answer. He buzzed again. Nothing. He leaned on the buzzer for a solid minute for the hell of it. Added a few more staccato stabs at it afterward.

A little girl's voice came over the speaker.

"I'm not allowed to open the door," she said.

"Hi, is Jax Hickey there?" asked Logan.

"I'm not allowed to open the door," the girl said again.

"Do you know where Jax is?"

"At the wedding," she said.

"The wedding? I'm supposed to be at the wedding too. Do you know where the wedding is?"

"At the park," she said.

"The park? Do you know which park? Where it is?"

There was silence a moment.

"Behind, um, behind, um, near, um, near the White House," she said.

"The White House?" said Logan. "The government building with the fountain and lots of stairs?"

"Yeah," she said.

The legislature building.

"Thank you very much," said Logan. "Good job. Don't open the door for anyone, just like dad said."

Logan climbed back in the tow truck and made his way down Jasper and then south to the legislature grounds downtown.

It was Saturday so the streets were quiet around the legislature. He drove into the park behind high windows and columns. There was no parking out front, but as Logan turned the corner, the long park space behind the legislature building was lined with expensive Lamborghinis, Hummers, Porsches. A red Dodge Viper parked diagonally to take up two spaces. A convertible Ferrari parked with its top down in a handicapped spot without any blue tag hanging from the rear-view mirror.

People sat in rows of seats draped with white covers tied in bows at the back. Flowers decorated a white arch over the aisle and a white gazebo where a priest stood marrying the happy couple. A little boy and girl chased each other with a balloon around the grassy park behind the seating area.

A few people turned their heads with pissed off expressions as they heard the tow truck rumble past. Then the bride and groom kissed and everybody stood and clapped. The happy couple were escorted to a table draped in a frilly white sheet with more flowers and a big book on top.

He found the little blue Roadster with white racing stripes parked diagonally across two handicapped spaces. The tow truck faced it head-on and there wasn't enough room to turn the truck around so Logan took another lap around the block to come at it from a better angle.

The gears ground as he shifted, and the tow truck belched out a cloud of black smoke as he accelerated. When he returned, he backed up until the tow bar nudged the front tires of the classic-looking Roadster. Across the field, a woman in a grey pantsuit and holding a large camera paraded the couple around the park with their families.

A man in a blue bow tie and sunglasses stepped out from the crowd. He wore a patterned dress shirt tucked into khaki shorts. Much of the wedding party were now turned around and looking at Logan.

"Do you have eyes?" he yelled. "Can't you see there's a wedding taking place?"

"I'll be out of your hair in a second," said Logan. He grabbed the wheel straps and jumped out of the truck.

"Whose car is this?" asked the guy.

"Jax Hickey," said Logan.

"Who?"

"Jax Hickey."

"Shouldn't he be here for this?"

"I don't care."

"Can this wait?"

"No," said Logan.

"Unbelievable," said the man. He stormed off back toward the wedding party. He detoured toward a visibly distressed bride and her angered husband who glared toward the tow truck. The first pecker-head held his arms up in reassuring gestures and then turned in to the crowd of people.

He talked to a different pecker-head, turning him by the shoulder and pointed at the tow truck.

The second pecker-head marched over to the sidewalk next to Logan. He also wore a powder blue shirt tucked into khaki shorts, with a sport coat over top. An apparent spray tan covered his face but left his eyelids pale like a frog's underbelly. Two young women who looked like aspiring reality show contestants followed behind him, clip clopping up and down on their high heels trying to keep up.

"What the fuck is this?" Hickey asked.

"I'm here for the car," said Logan.

"Excuse me?"

"Whatever," said Logan, brushing his way past Hickey. He crouched down by the passenger side wheel to lock the wheel bar in place and slipped on the wheel strap.

"Yeah pal," said Hickey. "I don't know who you think you are but you don't just tow away a 427 Cobra."

Logan stopped what he was doing and stood up.

"I'm sorry. What?" asked Logan.

"This car is worth more than your life."

"Jax," whined one of the ladies. She wore a black cocktail dress and a thin silver necklace. "What's going on?"

"Nothing," said Jax, maintaining eye contact with Logan. "He's confused."

Logan looked for something in Jax' eyes and didn't find it. Did this guy expect Logan to also pretend it's a 427 Cobra? Logan shook his head to snap himself back to reality and let out with it.

"That's not a 427 Cobra," said Logan, and turned away to walk around the driver's side tire.

Hickey followed him around to the other side of the car and crouched down next to Logan.

"Look pal," said Hickey. "You got the wrong guy. Why don't you get this trash heap out of here before you embarrass yourself?"

Logan flicked out the copy of the contract with Hickey's ID photocopied to it.

"Looks like you," said Logan, and resumed fastening the wheel strap.

"Jax," whined the other girl, gum in her mouth. "Do something."

Logan stood up and Jax blocked his path.

"Listen," said Jax. "I'm kind of somebody with his shit together. I'm a lawyer. You know that, right? You're some lowlife with a tow truck. Maybe you should be perfectly sure of what you're doing before you come blustering around here. I'm going to do you a favour. I'll give you a chance to get out of here before I fuck up your life worse than it already is."

By this time, the photographer and the married couple and members of their families had also gathered to see what the commotion was about.

"We're trying to take wedding photos," yelled the photographer, with emphasis on the last two words. "Get that junk out of here."

The bride looked like she was about to cry.

"Jax," whined the first girl again. "What's going on?"

"This lowlife thinks he can just tow away my Cobra," said Jax, pulling out his phone.

"That's not a 427 Cobra," repeated Logan.

Jax's cheeks flushed red.

"What is your problem, asshole?"

"It's a kit," said Logan.

"That car is worth more than your life," said Jax.

"That may be so," said Logan. "But it's only worth twenty grand." Logan pulled the contract out of his back pocket again.

"Twenty-one thousand, two hundred and twenty four dollars and fourteen cents, to be exact," he said.

"I'm calling the police," said Jax. He pressed his phone to his ear. "You see all these people? They're all lawyers and judges. You want to ruin the wedding of a judge's daughter? All these people will fuck your ass back to last Monday pro bono."

The heat rose into Logan's face. He walked back to the levers, pulled one, and started lifting the car.

"One, two, three, four," he counted under deep breaths.

"Dipshit," said Jax. "Stop what you're doing."

"Five, six, seven, eight," Logan continued.

"If you take this car," said Jax, his phone still pressed to his ear. "I will run you in for grand theft auto and you can sit in prison for as long of your loser life I feel like dragging it out for."

"Nine."

"I swear to God, if you lay another finger on my Cobra—"

"For the last goddamn time," said Logan. "That's not a Cobra."

Logan strode over and grabbed Jax by the bowtie, his other hand behind his neck.

"Look. Look at this," said Logan. He pointed Jax's head toward the car. "Looks at those side pipes. Look how shiny that chrome is. These girls could do their makeup in those pipes. The 427 Cobra did not come with shiny car show chrome like that. Now look at this."

He pulled Jax' head up and pointed it at the rear of the car.

"Look at that fucking obnoxious roll bar," said Logan. "It spans the whole rear of the car. If this were a real 427 Cobra, if it had a roll bar at all, it would be a single loop above the driver. I'm not here to entertain your delusional fantasies."

"Listen —"

"No, you listen to me, pecker-head," said Logan. He twisted the bowtie tighter in his hand until his knuckles dug into Jax's jugular. "Here's what you're going to do. You're going to back up and stand next to your girlfriends over there. Tell Betty and Veronica whatever you want. You can strut around and say tough guy things. Hold that phone up to your face and pretend you're talking to someone who gives a shit. I don't care. Mostly what you're going to do is stay the fuck out of my way and let me do my job. Understand?"

Jax spluttered and nodded his head. Logan let go and sent him staggering backward. He pulled another lever and the truck pulled the car closer to the back bumper.

"Jax," said one of the women. "Are you OK? What's going on?"

"The car will be stored on the lot for one month," Logan called out to Jax. "You can arrange payment with Ricky in that time."

Hickey made sniveling noises. The bride was furious. A few people gathered around Hickey to see if he was OK. Some faces peeked out from other clusters of people around the park to see what was going on.

Their heads turned to watch Logan tow the little roadster away down the street until he was gone around the corner.

He drove around the legislature building up to Jasper Avenue and back up to 118th Avenue. When he pulled into the alley behind the lot, Ricky and Tom were out back smoking. Once he reversed the little car into a space on the lot, Logan climbed out and walked over to the levers to lower the car. Something about Logan's face made Ricky raise an eyebrow.

"What the fuck happened to you?" asked Ricky. "Your face is all red."

"Got into a little argument," said Logan. Ricky and Tom both chuckled.

"He try and stop you from taking it?"

"More or less," said Logan. "He was yelling insults at me, which I was able to ignore for the most part. But he kept calling it a 427 Cobra and I snapped and there was a little dust up."

Ricky and Tom both laughed a little louder.

"It's about as authentic as a twelve of hearts," said Logan. "It was at a fancy wedding though. So you might get an angry phone call."

Ricky shrugged.

"That's fine," he said. "Come grab a beer."

They walked back to a little cooler by the back door of the shop. Ricky pulled a can of Gold Star out of the ice and handed it to Logan.

"Got any other jobs?" asked Logan. He cracked the tab open but didn't drink right away. "I could use the work."

"I imagine you could," said Ricky with an edge in his voice. "Those poker tables aren't going to play themselves."

Logan's face clouded but he didn't say anything.

"Yeah, there's a car," said Ricky. "I'm not sure I want to send you for this one. It's a bit dodgy. Hang on."

Ricky disappeared inside the pawn shop and went downstairs. A short while later Logan heard Ricky's cowboy boots clack back up the stairs and he came out the door with papers in his hand. He passed them to Logan. A Honda Civic. The signee was a Ms. Kimberly Houghten on the south side of town.

"What's the problem with it?"

"It's her boyfriend," said Ricky. "I never should have done the loan. This guy comes in with his girlfriend. Pretty sure he's a gang member. You know the type. Ball cap, face tattoos, sun glasses, lots of gold. They come in with her paperwork completed perfectly. Her ID, her three most recent pay stubs, last year's taxes. Everything. They made it impossible for me to not give the loan. The whole time she's signing the papers, he's sitting behind her not saying a word with a pissed off look on his face like someone slapped his cat. Once it's all done, I was kicking myself as soon as they walked out the door."

"And I guess he kicked her to the curb as soon as he got the car," said Logan.

"You know it. So the information on the contact there is fairly useless. Only proves I own the car. I don't want to have to send this to collections because she's not the bad guy here. But someone phoned me and said they saw a white Honda Civic in Chipperfield Court. Maybe go take a look. If it's the same car, maybe come get Tom to go with you. This guy's a pretty bad dude."

"I can do that," said Logan and he folded the papers and put them in his back pocket.

"How are you coming along with the Corvette?"

Logan looked away. Closed one eye and screwed up his mouth a little.

"I've been asking around," he said. "I talked to Kenny's daughter and his girlfriend. They don't know where the car is. I talked to his employee who drives a truck for him. He said he didn't know where it is. I believe him. The husband of the other woman who was killed wants to help me look for it so I guess it doesn't hurt to have another pair of eyes out there. I talked to one of Kenny's neighbours — Talia

Bodkins," said Logan with the same pinched nasal tone Talia's voice inspired. "She didn't see anything. She's a director for the Body, Mind, and Soul convention. It's for New Age health nuts."

Ricky nodded. Maybe he had heard of it. Maybe not.

"And she's also on the We Believe in 118 committee."

Ricky rolled his eyes.

"Those people asked me to put their 'We Believe in 118' sign in the shop window and then proceeded to inform me what a terrible person I am. I asked if any of them were prepared to give loans to any of the folks who come in here, if they would help out a drywall taper with some money to fix his truck. They called me a predator. I told them to get the fuck out of my store."

Ricky spat on the ground.

"They'll never be able to gentrify this neighborhood," he said. "Fix it up a bit maybe, but they can't change it. There's too many years of pain and anger. It seeps into the cracks of the walls, into the cement and the asphalt. Contaminates the ground like gasoline."

Ricky pulled out his wallet and thumbed out a hundred bucks and handed it to Logan.

As Logan was about to grab it, Ricky pulled it back.

"This is for rent," he said, eyebrows raised.

Logan reached for the bills. Ricky pulled it back again, looked Logan in the eye, and finally relinquished the bills into Logan's hand.

As Logan walked away, Ricky flicked his cigarette butt into the empty coffee can by the door. It made a sound. 'Tung.'

Tension took hold in Logan's chest as he sat on the number 4 bus. A tightness in his chest and shortness of breath. It stayed there, clenching at his middle all the way over the river and across the city and didn't let go until he walked into the front doors of Pulse Casino on the south side of town. Then he could breathe again. He gravitated to a Hold 'Em table full of oil field workers and once he sat down the muscles in his back relaxed. The oil field workers were wrapping up a stint of seven days off and looked like they hadn't slept for any of them. Living out of suitcases rumpled their clothes and their eyes sunk so deep in their faces they looked out from far behind their cheekbones.

Everything inside the casino's walls moved lockstep in time to a steady rhythm. The servers made their rounds, starting at the table games and then worked their way back through the VLT machines in an orderly formation. Jackpot sounds jangled in the background. At the top of the hour, winning Keno numbers blinkered onto a large screen as new security staff came on shift and the day shift left. Right on time. All around, the numbers played themselves out.

Round and round, the big blind pulled the little blind, their gravity dragging along stacks of chips in their wake. The chips sailed off of orbit in trajectories determined by the play of the cards.

Two aces drifted over from the dealer and into Logan's hand. A shade under fifty percent chance of winning against six other players. Then a partial straight came up in the flop - Nine, Ten, Jack — which didn't bode well, but two of the guys folded to keep Logan's odds just under fifty-fifty. Chips piled up in the centre of the table.

A three of spades flipped over on the turn. Logan went all in.

Then an ace turned up on the river. Logan doubled his money and pulled the stacks of chips toward himself.

The other guys at the table nodded in agreement with the order of things.

Servers did their rounds. Ringing sounds rang. The dealer shuffled and dealt.

Then for the rest of the evening, garbage cards lined up to enter Logan's hands. A three-ten. Two-five. Four-nine. As the blinds circled the table, Logan's stack of chips whittled down lower and lower.

A swirling sensation wavered out from the table as Logan's chips got caught in the tide and sailed away from him. The room began to spin.

Like a whirlpool, round and round it went until Logan threw down a three-eight and got up from the table. The swirling momentum of the blinds cast him off in a new trajectory. He cashed in his last remaining chip at the teller for twenty dollars and left the casino.

Logan walked. West at first, then north, then east, then south, then north again, spiraling inward on downtown like a big blind. The buildings were dilapidated at first, as though the apocalypse happened a long time ago and nobody noticed, and everybody kept continuing on with their lives. Then the buildings got nicer the closer he got to downtown.

He was thinking of something. Of what, he wasn't sure. Not the money. Not the poker. Something else. It stuck somewhere in his stomach and he walked and walked trying to work it out. As his feet stepped forward it felt less like he was walking and more like the Earth rolled underneath him. The sky turned to its gritty tangerine colour, and then dark blue with a long strip of purple along the horizon. And then it went dark.

He became aware of people talking around him and looked up to find himself in a trendy district of bars and restaurants off Jasper Avenue. What brought him there, he wasn't sure. People mingled around patio fire-tables, and others emerged from basement lounges under sloping canopies over the stairs. People crowded the sidewalk and Logan weaved between them.

Patrons in the window of a wine bistro looked him up and down from behind the window. He looked down at rust stains flecked across his jeans and he turned around. He passed a resto-lounge where a group of young friends laughed and drank colourful drinks. A muscular young man heaved one of the girls over his shoulder and they squealed and cheered. Further along, he came upon a pub called the District Taphouse and walked inside.

He sat at the bar under exposed light bulbs in wire frames, their filaments casting an orange pall on the room.

The bartender, a young man in a railroad cap, asked Logan what he wanted to drink.

"Gold Star," said Logan.

"We don't carry Gold Star," said the bartender, as though Logan had asked for pornography.

"What do you got?" asked Logan.

The bartender rolled his eyes and in a monotone recited a list of beers that sounded like shipyards and national parks.

"A lager," said Logan.

The bartender recommended one.

"It's nine dollars," the bartender warned.

"That's fine," said Logan. The bartender poured it and Logan put a ten on the bar.

All the walking across the city set into Logan's bones and he leaned forward on the bar to take a breath. The beer was good. Crisp and refreshing. He closed his eyes as he retraced his steps from the casino to where he was now. He replayed his thoughts and held each one up in his mind to ask if it was the thing bothering him.

He kept his eyes closed as he saw the faces of the rig workers at the poker table. He saw the darkened windows of derelict buildings along his walk downtown. He saw the face of Alexis at the Take Five shoveling pancakes into her face. He saw the QR code stuck to the blood spattered wall in Kenny Prince's house. He saw the single mom driving away in her minivan. He saw Clifford smoking dope in his fiance's house with blood smeared all over the walls. None of these seemed to be the thing gnawing at him.

A laugh filled the room. A distinct, pinched nasally sort of laugh. Logan opened his eyes and looked over the bar to the other side of the room and surveyed the booths along the exposed brick wall at the back. And there she was. Talia Bodkins sat in a booth with a group of people. She cocked her head back and gave a full-bodied laugh to the world.

15

Talia's laugh cut through all the music and chatter around the bar. Two other women and two men sat with her. The men gestured with their skinny arms, their hands grasping at invisible concepts in the air. They were on a roll. They wore plaid shirts with the sleeves rolled up below the elbow. One of the men wore a neatly trimmed, spherical beard and a mustache with the ends curled up. The women wore sharp blazers and maintained an aloof air about them as they listened to the guys talk. One of the women cast her eyes downward, looking vaguely offended by what one of the men was saying but also with the corners of her mouth pinched upward, perhaps also privately enjoying whatever it was as well.

Talia moved a cloth napkin from her lap to the table and excused herself. Logan watched her walk across the room to the washroom. A waiter cleaned the table while she was away. When Talia re-emerged, Logan kept his head down. She wore a short grey-blue dress, the colour of smoke from a blown-out match, and she drifted with an unhurried swagger back to the booth.

The other women stood up to let her back in the booth and they continued with their conversation and laughed some more. After another drink, the men acted bigger and louder. It was around then the ladies gave polite goodbyes. Talia stood up and hugged each of them. The group left and Talia stayed behind alone in the booth.

She ordered a martini from the waiter and scrolled through her phone.

Logan picked up his beer, walked over and slid into the booth opposite her.

"Oh my God," she said. "What are you doing here?"

"I was having a drink over there, looked over, and I saw you," said Logan.

"Small world," she said.

"It's about the right size."

"And what are you up to this fine evening?"

"Making the rounds," he said. "You?"

"I guess you could say I had a casual meeting with some work friends."

"The best kind of meeting."

"The martinis help, at least," she said. "How's your investigation going?"

She enunciated each syllable of 'investigation' and shimmied with her shoulders as she lifted her martini glass to her lips.

"It's coming along," said Logan. "You haven't heard anything since we talked last, have you?"

"All's quiet," she said, lifting her glass to her mouth. She smiled and touched the rim of the glass with her teeth while she thought of something. She regained her composure.

"Do you have any leads?" she asked.

"A couple," said Logan. "We'll see where they go."

"What are your leads?" Talia asked. "I'll keep it a secret. Honest. No one gets anything out of me. I'm like a steel trap."

"Because you're sharp and quick? Or cold and ruthless?"

"I'm touchy," she said. "And I bite."

A flick of her eyebrow lashed at Logan. She pulled the olive spear out of her glass. It had two olives on it and she slid the first olive off between her teeth.

"You guys looked like you're celebrating something," said Logan.

"We're bringing James on board," said Talia. "Although maybe he's bringing us on board and we don't realize it yet. He's created an app that's a hub for all the healthy living and spiritual gurus. The gurus upload videos of guided meditations, or exercises, or cooking recipe instructions and interact with followers. You can track your meditations and exercises. Receive daily messages and whatnot."

"And people pay for that?"

"To feel reassured, motivated, and part of a community that's connected to a higher power?" asked Talia. "Oh yeah. They pay for that."

"I could use some of that," said Logan. "Do you have any spiritual advice for me?"

"Live in the now," she said. Her voice disintegrated with vocal fry at the back of her throat as she spoke. She swirled and slung the last of her martini into her mouth. "Isn't that what they all say?"

"When else am I going to live?"

"I don't think we really live in the present," she said.

"No?" asked Logan. "When do we live?"

"Like, if I ask you who you are — who you really are — would you say this is it?" She gestured with her hand up and down at Logan. "Is this the truest version of you? Detective Claybourne doing whatever it is we're doing in this cookie cutter boho-industrial brew pub?"

"It's not?" said Logan.

"Of course it's not."

She stared off into her glass and dropped the olive spear into it.

"We just say and do whatever works in the moment," she said. "But it's not really us. It's our past that sets our course in life."

"But if you truly live in the now, doesn't that mean you're tapped into a truer version of yourself?"

"Maybe," she said. "I've tried them all. Yoga, transcendental meditation, reiki, Zen. You want to know the best one?"

Logan lifted a beer in a small salute that asked her to continue.

"Driving on the highway alone at night," she said. "When you're alone and there's no traffic, it's like another dimension. Just some music and your thoughts. After a while you tap into a different part of yourself. A part of yourself that exists outside of time. You have a conversation with that part of yourself. It's honest and it's totally divorced from 'the now' but it feels more real."

"I think I know what you mean," said Logan. "You should teach that on your app."

She stared into her glass but shook her head and snapped back to reality.

"I'm talking too much and embarrassing myself, and you're not even telling me anything about your investigation," she said. "Come on, you can share something. A little hint. You must have a lead about who killed my neighbour? I'm distraught thinking about what happened to the poor man."

"Now, now. There's no need to get theatrical."

She smiled a cheeky smile.

"There's been another murder," said Logan. "A woman in her 30s. We think the same person did it."

Talia wiggled in her seat as though to settle herself into the story.

"That's awful," she said. "What do you know so far?"

"There's not too much else," he said. "Do you know much about QR Codes? Do you use them much in your work?"

"They'll be on some signage around the convention centre," she said. "You point your phone at them and they'll open up whatever website. Here, look. This bar has a QR code for their menu."

She pointed to a QR code at the edge of the table along the wall. She pulled out her phone and scanned it, touched a prompt on her screen and the bar's menu on their website appeared on her phone. The words were too large and disappeared off either side of her phone.

"Of course, it's not optimized for mobile because restaurant owners will spend a hundred thousand dollars on a vintage cappuccino machine but will insist on making their website themselves on blogtoilet dot com or whatever. Why? What is your issue with QR codes?"

"There were prominent QR codes at both crime scenes," said Logan.

"Did you scan them?"

"Yes," said Logan. "At Kenny's. Nothing comes up. Just a screen that says 'This page has expired.'"

"This is juicy," she said. "What else are you holding out on me?"

"I don't have much else, I'm afraid," said Logan.

"Grisly, though, isn't it?" She gave a shiver. "Creepy to think someone's out there doing this. Makes me want to lock the door, turn out the lights, and hide under a blanket."

"I wouldn't worry. I'm sure the murder was targeted."

"Come to think of it, living in hiding is still preferable to living next to that thing so long as I get some peace and quiet. That's horrible, isn't it? I'm sorry. That's terrible. You must think I'm a total bitch. Well, I guess I am. Oh well."

They both chuckled.

"Was he really that bad?"

"Oh my God," she said. ""We have a little old lady in our building. Her name's Harriet. She's like eighty years old. She was just walking down the street and Kenny grabbed his crotch and yelled at her asking if she wanted 'the time of her life.'"

The both chuckled some more.

"She called the police, but nothing happened of course."

"Aw, Harriet," said Logan.

"Another time, the police dropped him off at home. Heaven knows why. And he was wasted. And he got out of the police car and his pants fell down and he had no idea. Then as they're about to drive away he chases after them with his ass hanging out saying, 'Wait! I forgot my crack pipe!' And they opened the door and let him dig out his crack pipe."

Logan laughed. It stayed in him and he couldn't look her in the eye, and he ducked his head down closer to the table as he laughed and tried to collect himself.

"It's not funny," she said.

"I'm sorry," said Logan. "That's truly terrible."

Then they both looked at each other and laughed. The waiter came to check on them but left them alone for the time it took to collect themselves.

"You're not so angry, are you?" she said.

"I guess I have a short fuse sometimes," he said. He looked down at the table and felt his jacket pockets. Then he stopped and looked up at her. "Why would you say that?"

"Say what?"

"Why would you say 'I'm not so angry'?"

"I just said, you don't seem angry," she said.

"But that doesn't make sense. Why would I be angry?" he said, beginning to make himself angry. Heat filled his face.

She shook her head and snapped her mouth shut.

"I wanted to ask you something," said Logan. "Last time I saw you, as I was leaving, you said 'That would be a gamble.' I felt like you had a tone."

"I'm not sure what you mean," said Talia.

"Your receptionist thought it was funny," he said.

"I'm not sure what you're talking about," she said, looking away. She turned her head as far as she could to avoid Logan's face. She picked up the olive spear and sucked the other olive into her mouth.

"You don't remember?" asked Logan. "It was in the reception area. I said I hoped finding the car would lead to the killer, and you said, 'Hopefully your gamble pays off.' You and your receptionist seemed to think that was really funny."

She shrank in her seat. She moaned.

"Logan," she whined and followed it with a groan. He waited.

"Logan," she repeated in the same whiny voice. "You're so cringey."

"What?"

"Logan, don't make this awkward. We should just relax and have a good time."

"Make what awkward?"

"You," she said. "You are making all of this awkward."

"Making all of what awkward?"

"I have no idea what you're talking about," she said. She sat up straight again. "I have a question for you though."

"What?"

"Do you know how to steal a car?"

"You're changing the subject."

"I don't even know what you're talking about. But do you know how to steal a car?"

"Depends on what type it is."

"I want to steal a car."

"You want to steal a car."

"Yes." Her eyes lit up at the idea.

"But I don't want to steal a car. I want you to tell me what was so funny that time I was at your office."

"Oh stop. Come on," she said, leaning in. A crazed look filled her eye. "It will be fun."

"Why would I steal a car?"

"To live in the now!" she said. She swayed as she spoke and laughed to herself.

"You need to go to bed," he said.

"Are you flirting with me?"

"No, I'm not. I'm asking how you seem to know things about me and you're talking about stealing cars."

She lowered her chin and looked up at him with an eyebrow pointed at him.

"I know you're a repo man," she said.

"How do you know that?"

"Doesn't matter," she said.

"I think it does matter, actually," said Logan.

She shook her head no.

"Just tell me," said Logan.

"Not until we steal a car," she said.

"I'm not stealing anything," said Logan. "Do you want to repo a car? Is that it? If we repoed a car, will you tell me how you know all this about me?"

She beamed a bright smile and nodded.

"Tomorrow?" asked Logan.

"Right now."

Logan and Talia tumbled into the back of a black taxi. Logan gave the driver directions to the pawn shop and when he did, the cabbie took a second to turn around to inspect the both of them.

Talia flopped over in the back seat and laid her head down in Logan's lap. She sneered at the driver.

"We're kind of in a hurry," she snarled, and then laughed. She sat up, dug through her purse and produced a small vial of pills. She shook a couple out into her hand and popped them into her mouth. She then pulled out her lipstick and refreshed the dark burgundy colour on her lips.

"This is going to be so much fun," she said.

"You think so," said Logan, looking straight ahead.

Talia leaned into the side of Logan's face.

"Oh honey, don't be grumpy," she said, and gave his cheek a pat. "I really appreciate you taking me on a ride-along."

She sat up and leaned forward.

"We're repo men," she shouted at the driver. "We're important for the economy. Without us, there'd be no consequences for people living beyond their means. We're the ice cold slap of reality."

She slapped the back of the driver's seat as she spoke. The cabbie ignored her. She slumped back in her seat with a boozy smile on her face.

When they arrived at the pawn shop she paid the driver and Logan walked her toward the back lot.

"There's a couple of pitbulls here," he said. "Don't freak out and you'll be fine. They'll run up and bark at you but that's it. Just don't scream or run away or anything like that."

Logan unlocked the gate and Trixie and Dixie charged toward them - all teeth and drool and snarl. Talia stepped behind Logan and grabbed his shirt. She raised a knee defensively. Logan talked the dogs down with kissy noises until they settled and they walked together to the tow truck. She stood in front of it aghast.

"What the hell is this thing?"

"Tow truck."

"Does it run?"

They climbed in, Logan turned the ignition and the tow truck shuddered to life. Talia slapped both hands onto the dashboard as she laughed and then wiped her hands on Logan's shirt. She bent forward with her head by her knees and clapped her hands.

"This is amazing," she said.

He wrestled the stick into first gear and the truck lurched forward and Logan pulled it out of the lot.

"What kind of car are we getting?"

"White Honda Civic. One sec," said Logan. He jumped out and locked the gate behind them and climbed back in. "Here's the thing. This guy is supposed to be a pretty bad dude. So please just do what I say. And if anything happens, stay inside the truck and lock the door."

"Oooh, danger," she said. "Exciting."

"Yeah, it's a real treat," said Logan.

"Who is the guy?"

"Some gangster type," said Logan. "Ricky didn't want to do the loan. He knew better, but this guy came in with his girlfriend. They had all the paperwork filled out perfectly. In her name. She had two pieces of ID, three most recent pay stubs for her. They made it impossible for Ricky to not give them a loan."

"Where does she live?"

"I'm sure she's not in the picture anymore," said Logan. "These guys ditch them as soon as they get the money or the car or whatever. Someone saw the car outside this guy's house and told Ricky where it was. It's a townhouse in Chipperfield Court."

Chipperfield Court was a complex of townhouses in the northeast that took up four square blocks. Logan pulled into the road that looped around the townhouses. Some had tinfoil in the windows. Others had furniture in the front yard. They drove by several vehicles well beyond their home's tax bracket. A patch of grass that was supposed to be a playground served as a parking lot for several homes' secondary vehicles. A new truck here, a Mustang there, as well as various other cars.

At the corner of the road, they came upon the white Civic in front of one of the townhouses. Logan pulled ahead of it and reversed back until the tow bar nudged the front tires.

"Quiet," said Logan, holding a finger to his lips. "Don't close your door all the way."

She got out and circled around the front of the truck to meet him by the control levers.

"What can I do?" she asked.

"I'm going to lock the tow bar on it and put these straps on the wheels. Once I have the straps on, I'll point to you. Then you can push this lever. That will lift the car up. Then pull this lever. That will bring the car closer to the truck. When I hold my hand up, push the lever back."

Logan crouched down and clamped the tow bar in place. As he reached for the first tire strap a screen door slammed shut.

"Hey you motherfucker," a man's voice shouted.

Talia gave a short, sharp squeal.

He wore a white tank top and boxer shorts and bounded down the front steps with an aluminum baseball bat in his right hand. Logan sprang up and edged his way back toward Talia.

"I gotta take the car, man," said Logan. "No payments have been made."

"Unhook the car," the man said. "Unhook it now."

"Logan, he's got a bat," said Talia, and she covered her nose and mouth with her hands. Logan held his palm up to Talia and kept his eyes on the guy with the bat.

The bat wavered in circles by his knees as his grip clenched and loosened on the handle.

"Just doing my job, man," said Logan. "It'll be in storage and you can go in and make payment arrangements to get it back."

"Unhook it now or I'll beat you where you fucking stand," said the guy.

"Sure, no problem," said Logan. "We can totally make an arrangement where you keep the car. Put the bat down. Christ."

"Like what?" he asked.

"The car's not even in your name, man," said Logan. "Like, if we at least had the car in your name we could probably work something out."

"I don't have any credit," he said.

"Ricky's pretty shifty," said Logan. "I'm sure he can work around that. You just pay a bit more interest or something. You have some ID?"

"My probation card," the guy said.

"That'll probably work," said Logan. "I have some papers in the truck. Let's fill them out."

"Unhook the car first," said the guy.

"Sure," said Logan, and he knelt down and unlocked the tow bar from the wheels.

"Grab your ID and let's figure this thing out."

The guy walked backwards into the house, keeping an eye on Logan as he leaned on the back of the truck. Talia stood up bolt straight by the lift levers.

Logan leaned into the driver's side door and grabbed some papers from under the seat.

"Logan," she whisper-yelled. "What are you doing?"

Logan ignored her and followed the guy toward the townhouse.

The guy disappeared into the front door. Logan waited five seconds and then ran back to the car. He ducked down and locked the tow bar back in place. No time for straps. He pointed at Talia and then pointed 'up,up' while mouthing the words.

She pushed the lever and the front end of the Civic lifted toward the sky.

The man came bounding out of the front door, pulling his pants up and struggling to fix his belt.

"You're fucking dead," he said.

Logan jumped in the tow truck's driver's seat. Talia ran around the front of the truck but by then the man had come closer with the baseball bat and she couldn't reach the passenger side door.

She ran back to the Civic. She opened the driver's side door and climbed in.

"Go! Go!" she yelled.

Logan popped the clutch but the truck stalled. It shuddered briefly and went quiet.

"You're both fucking dead," the man yelled. He swung the bat at the Civic and smashed the passenger side window.

"Go! Go!" Talia yelled again.

"I'm trying," Logan yelled into the steering wheel. The guy whacked the bat against the roof of the car.

"Get out of there you fucking bitch," the guy said.

Logan flicked the ignition off and on again. He popped the clutch, the truck coughed out a plume of black smoke, and they rolled forward.

The guy ran up along side of the truck and took a whack at the back end of it.

"Put my car down now."

The car's back tire hit a pot hole. The car leaned out of the tow bar, the passenger side tire lifted out of it by several inches as the car threatened to topple out entirely.

Logan braked them to a crawl and the car fell back into the tow bar.

The bat swung down into the front windshield, leaving a golf ball-sized hole.

Talia screamed.

"Logan," she yelled. "Get us out of here!"

"I'm trying," Logan yelled but stayed at school-zone speed and watched out his side view mirror at the car bouncing on the bars.

Logan could hear a stream of curse words interrupted by the 'chunk' sound of each blow of the bat onto the car.

Eventually the man ran out of energy and stood in the middle of the road holding the bat out to his side.

"I know what you look like. You listen to me. I'm coming for you!" he yelled.

Logan pulled the tow truck out onto the main road and lumbered along before pulling down another residential street, one that was wide and quiet. He took a few more turns until he found a secluded spot where he would still have a good view of anyone pulling up.

Talia climbed out of the Civic.

"Holy shit," she said. "This is your job?"

She got into the passenger seat of the tow truck and watched out the back window as Logan lowered the battered Civic down to the street. He fastened the straps around the front tires and lifted it back up again. He got back in the truck and they made their way back to Champion City Pawn.

It was the middle of the night. Neither said anything the whole way back to the pawn shop. Instead, they watched the way the lights reflected off the street and got lost in their own thoughts.

The truck seemed to drive itself and they floated down the road. There were no other cars and the sky was pitch black. The only sound was the chugging of the truck engine and the tires wheeling over wet asphalt.

When they arrived back at the shop, the pitbulls barked and scrambled around the truck. Logan reversed the car into a space, unhooked it, and then parked the tow truck along the back fence. Talia didn't react much to the pitbulls this time.

She tapped into her phone and summoned a car. They waited in silence until the car arrived and ferried them back to her condo building.

16

Talia flicked on the light and dragged her feet around the kitchen. Whatever poise she carried during the day had evaporated now from a combination of booze and exhaustion.

Her place was clean. A lot of white panels and sharp lines. The kitchen smelled faintly of ginger. She grabbed a couple glasses from the cupboard and crouched down behind the kitchen island and pulled up a bottle of gin.

Logan perused her bookshelf as he walked by it before standing at the patio window. He looked down at Kenny Prince's house.

"That house is so eerie now," she said, handing him a gin and tonic. She gave a little shiver.

She walked to the living room and stretched out on the couch.

"Well your job isn't boring," she said. "I'll give you that."

She took a sip of her drink and let out a long breath.

"I should go to bed," she said.

"Hey."

She hummed a response.

"You said you'd tell me how you know things about me," he said.

She closed her eyes.

"I really don't," she said. "I was drunk back there. I don't really know much about you."

"Come on," said Logan.

She grimaced and made an exasperated noise.

"I'm tired," she said.

"Come on," said Logan again.

Her eyes remained shut tight while she went over something in her mind. When she opened her eyes again they were softer and they locked on to Logan's. She took a drink.

"There's a list," she said. "You're on the list."

"What list?"

"A list people subscribe to where information is kept and stored on other people."

"Can I see the list?"

She bit her bottom lip and smiled as she shook her head no.

"That's not fair," he said. "I should be able to see what people are saying about me."

She shook her head no again, more slightly this time.

"Who runs this list?" asked Logan.

"I don't know," she said. "There are people with invitation privileges but I don't think there's any one owner. And eventually this list might die off and a new list starts somewhere else. And people will copy the data from this list and move it to the next one."

"Don't you think that's kind of psycho?" he asked.

An arrogant tone affected her face.

"No," she said. "I think it's normal."

"Normal how?"

"I'm on the We Believe in 118 committee," she said. "We're committed to improving this part of the city. Understanding the people who live here is a good thing. Knowing the community is a good thing. It's due diligence at bare minimum."

She said it as though it were both obvious and she was doing everyone a favour.

"The committee runs the list?"

"Oh no," she said. "The list is much bigger than that. Way bigger. We just subscribe to it. I think everyone on the committee subscribes to it. Most of us do, anyway."

"You can't do this to me," said Logan. "You have to at least let me see what people have written about me. Don't I deserve at least that much?"

She slid down further on the couch so her head was on the arm rest. She shook her head no again and smiled. She beckoned him with her finger.

"What?"

"Come here," she said. She pulled her feet up on the couch to make room.

Logan moved over and sat on the couch. Talia bit her bottom lip and beckoned him further with her finger.

"You have to let me see this list," said Logan.

"OK," she said. "You have to do something for me first."

"What?"

She lowered her eyelids and beckoned him some more with her finger. Logan laid down next to her.

"I just —" he started. She held a finger up to his mouth.

"Don't say anything," she said. "Don't make any sounds."

She moved his hand onto her lower back but turned his face at an angle from hers, resisting.

"It's OK," she said. "I know I'm a bitch. You don't have to like me. Just do what I tell you."

Their clothes came off. Talia gave him specific instructions on what to do and in what order. Where to kiss and where to touch. His movements were firm but cold and mechanical according to her directions.

She moved his hands where she wanted them to go. Logan shifted and cradled and pushed like an elaborate piece of furniture or exercise machinery. Once he had repeated these movements enough times for her satisfaction, she took him by the hand and led him to her bedroom.

When Logan awoke he lay flat on his back and stared up at the ceiling. Something about his being awake caused Talia to stir. She sat up in bed with the sheets covering her and looked straight ahead, bracing herself for whatever came next.

"Let's see this list," said Logan.

She turned to protest but his face said he was serious. She put her head back against the headboard and shut her eyes tight.

"Logan," she whined. "You're so embarrassing."

She pulled a laptop off the nightstand and opened it up on her lap.

"I shouldn't have said anything," she muttered to herself as she typed onto the keyboard and called up the list. When it loaded she sat further up against the headboard and took a deep breath.

"Your feelings are going to get hurt," she said.

Logan nodded and motioned for the laptop with a wave of his hand.

She searched for his name and scrolled down to the entry on Logan and passed her laptop over to him. After he took it, she rubbed the corners of her eyes, massaged the bridge of her nose, and ran her fingers through her hair.

It was a spreadsheet saved to the cloud on the internet. Pages and pages of thousands of people were listed. Various colours bordered different cells.

A thick black box bordered Logan's name and information. A list of details of Logan's life followed after his name. The entries were in different fonts and written in different cadences, compiled by various people Logan had crossed paths with throughout life.

It started with, "Logan Claybourne: DNH."

"What does DNH mean?" he asked.

"Do Not Hire," said Talia. "That's what the black border means. 'Do not hire for any management position or salary that pays over fifty grand a year.'"

"So you people canceled any opportunity I might have and I never would have known? I could have spent the rest of my life applying for jobs for nothing."

"I didn't put that," she said, lifting her shoulder up to her cheek. She moved on from the subject. "There are other border colours. Red is for rapists, pedophiles, or other problematic sex issues. Orange is weird issues with women. Green is for when they got caught embezzling or doing something illegal at work but were never charged. Yellow means they're racist but a lot of us have stopped using that one. It became a flag for other racists to seek each other out. They were using it to network."

Logan continued reading the entries by his name.

"Repo man for his brother-in-law. Insane gambling addiction. Serious anger management issues. Probably some other significant mental health issues as well."

A link next to the basic entry led to another sheet with more detailed entries about him, which read like a gossip forum.

"He spent all day gambling at the Klondike Casino," one entry read. "He didn't even eat. When he lost all his chips at the poker table he quietly stood up and walked to the casino washroom and cried in a bathroom stall. Not sitting on the toilet, mind you. He collapsed onto the floor of the bathroom stall and was blubbering on the floor. Kicking, crying, snot coming out of his nose, complete breakdown. Eventually security came and knocked on the bathroom stall. As soon as Logan heard them, he shot up off the floor. Went dead quiet. Sat up on the toilet for half a minute collecting himself. Then he comes out of the bathroom stall with a smile on his face. Says 'hello' to the security. Washes his hands in the sink humming a little song. The security guards are a little stunned because they're expecting a confrontation. So now they don't know what to do. 'Everything OK?' asks one of the security guards. 'Doing good. How you boys doing tonight?' says Logan. The guards stand around looking at each other. Logan hummed a happy tune while he dried his hands then walked out, sat at a VLT machine and spends the rest of the night dropping all of his money in it. Crazy gambling problem. I'm kind of scared of him. I think he's psycho."

Logan let his head fall and picked it back up again. Took a breath and moved on to the next entry.

"His sister Clare did really good at school. When they were kids he spazzed out like he always does and made his little sister run away from home with him. They lived on the streets together. Pretty nice brother to make his sister homeless with him. She has her own issues too and has really struggled, no thanks to Logan."

"What the fuck," said Logan. He turned to Talia. "We came from a really bad home. Why doesn't somebody write that?"

He moved on to the next entry.

"Works as a repo-man for his brother-in-law, which is DISGUSTING. I don't know how you could live with yourself taking away vehicles from poor families who have put so much money in to them and are already struggling."

And more.

"Little fucking shit would walk around with his sister stealing tools from one pawn shop and pawning them at another. He'd even peel the stickers off in the pawn shop and pawn it back to the same shop if the broker wasn't paying attention. He's a fucking little thief."

And more.

"Caught him digging through the dumpster behind our building. Super gross. Keep an eye out if he's in your back alley LOL."

And more.

"I gave him an eviction notice (after he gambled all his money away, of course) and he just walked away from the place. Didn't take a single stick of furniture with him. CREEPY. Kind of psychotic if you ask me."

And on.

"Saw him sleeping on a bench until a cat came along and fought him for the bench and he LOST TO THE CAT and slept on the ground while the cat took the bench. What a loser."

And on.

"You guys are mean. I think he has some kind of trauma. Obviously you don't want to hire him and he's psycho and weird and everything, but you're kind of showing your ass in the way you talk about him. Maybe look at yourselves."

Then below it—

"I have looked at myself. I have a job and a family. I have a house and I go on vacation. I put my life together. Logan's an asshole."

Then another.

"He's always saying 'You dig?' like a jazz scatting cool cat or something."

"I was wondering why people kept saying that to me," said Logan. "I didn't think I did that."

Logan backed out of that screen back to the general list of names with various coloured boxes everywhere.

Many names had various emojis next to them.

"What do these emojis mean?"

"A deck of cards means they're not playing with a full deck," said Talia. "Like, they're kind of dumb. Drinks go next to alcoholics."

"Present company excluded, I suppose?" said Logan.

"You know it," she said, with a sassy shrug of her shoulder.

"The pipe goes next to druggies. A red stripe is a suspected spy or government informant. A brown star goes next to girls who will take it in the ass. The eggplant goes next to guys who have big dicks. Here."

She took the laptop and put an eggplant next to Logan's name.

"It's only fair," she said. "There's lots of emojis people use. I don't even know what all of them mean."

"Can't you just delete me?"

"Nope, you can only delete entries people make about yourself. People can go into the edit history and if you've deleted information about someone else you get banned from the list. And I'm not giving up this list for anybody."

"How much does it cost to subscribe?"

"You pay in crypto-currency. It works out to about sixty dollars a month, which is more than worth it for the entertainment value let alone the practical applications."

"Can you invite me?"

"I don't have invitation privileges," she said. "Sorry."

Logan searched for Kenny Prince and the screen scrolled down to his entry.

"EVIL," it read in capital letters. "Kenny Prince is a criminal, a drug addict, he uses prostitutes. He will urinate off the back of his hot tub in his backyard because he's too drunk or lazy to go inside. He smells like actual shit from his septic tank service. He has the only house blocking Phase 4 development to improve that part of Eastwood. It's like he's deliberately thumbing his nose at the community."

"I suppose you wrote that?"

She didn't need to respond.

"Seems he was a thorn in the side for development in the area as well?"

"We offered him amounts far and away more than what his house is worth and he refused," she said.

"So," said Logan. "In a roundabout kind of way, someone might interpret you as having a motive?"

"It's not illegal to put someone on a list," she said.

"Did you think something might happen to him when you wrote that?"

"This list exists to inform others," she said. "But, no, I have no control over what other people do."

"I'm not sure how to take that," said Logan.

"I don't know how else to put it," she said. "I don't know who killed Kenny Prince."

She crossed her arms and drew in closer over Logan's shoulder.

"I shouldn't have let you see this in the first place," she said. "Can I have it back now?"

"One more," said Logan, and he searched for Brooke Esterly. The screen zoomed down to her name.

"She was nothing before she met me," the passage read. "I gave her everything and she has the nerve to file for divorce and take me for half of everything I built up with my bare hands? She's nuts. She's mentally unwell. Schizo-affective, ADHD, bi-polar, you name it. She's a drain on the system just collecting welfare. Her brain is broken and she's a thief that took me for everything I've built up."

"Jilted ex-husband," said Talia.

"Do you know her?" asked Logan.

"Never heard of her," she said.

Logan handed the laptop back to Talia. He slid back down in bed and resumed looking at the ceiling with his hands folded on his stomach.

"I'm sorry," said Talia. "You shouldn't have seen that."

"It's fine," said Logan.

"Maybe you can keep your nose clean and one day you'll meet someone with invitation privileges," she said.

"It's fine," Logan repeated.

"Do you have any questions?"

"I have a lot of questions," said Logan. "But I can't think of the words."

Logan closed his eyes but remained awake. Talia tapped away at something on her computer. The sun gradually filtered into her bedroom. A vibrating and the blaring Latin pop song form Logan's phone erupted from the floor next to the bed.

He stretched over the side of the bed and pulled it out of his jeans pocket. It was a text message from Cliff.

"I'm going to kill myself," it read.

"Fuck," said Logan. "I gotta go."

Talia didn't say anything.

Logan got out of bed, pulled on his clothes, and left without either of them saying anything else.

17

Logan went home and put on some coffee. He took a shower while it brewed and when he got out he ate some toast and eggs. He practiced shuffling the top card of the deck to the second position, then the third, then the fourth, and back to the top while he drank his cup of coffee. If Clifford killed himself in that time, there was nothing that could be done. Cliff would have to wait until Logan was good and ready.

When he finished his cup of coffee he phoned Cliff.

"Cliff, what's going on?"

"I can't breathe," he said. "I feel like I'm drowning. Everything keeps pushing me down."

"You should talk to someone," said Logan.

"I'm talking to you," said Cliff. "Can you come over please? I'm scared of what I'm going to do."

"Sure," he said. "Hang on."

Logan jogged down the apartment building stairwell and outside. He ducked into a Vietnamese sandwich restaurant and picked up subs for himself and Cliff and walked up to Cliff's house.

When he got there, a large 'For Sale' sign stood on the front lawn of the house with a second smaller sign hanging under it listing the house as a foreclosure. A photo on the sign showed a real estate agent named Darcy Hannigan with white, straight teeth and slick hair. He flashed a million dollar smile so lustrous it was probably insured.

Logan tried the door but it was locked. The curtains were drawn across the living room window and when Logan rang the door bell, Cliff peeked out from the end of the curtains at a sideways angle, with his back against the wall. When Cliff came around and opened the door, the air was thick with pot smoke.

"Sandwich," said Logan. "I didn't put any cilantro on it. Not sure how you feel about cilantro."

"Thank you so much," said Cliff. "I haven't eaten in days."

Clifford's eyes were blood red and baggy but he spoke fluidly.

When they rounded the corner to the living room, Logan saw three heavy knives stuck out of the wall above the couch. Several more holes tore up the drywall around them.

"I hope you weren't redecorating on my account," said Logan.

"I was practicing knife throwing," said Cliff with his mouth full. "They're taking the house from me so I don't care."

He devoured half the sandwich while Logan was still pulling his own out of the bag.

"Thank you so much," said Cliff. "This sandwich is amazing."

"What's going on?" asked Logan. "You OK?"

"I'm not in a good place, man," said Cliff. "A real estate agent came around and said he's putting the house up for sale. I tried to tell him he can't do that. It's me and Brooke's house. He told me I have to move out. It's our house though, man. He can't just do that, can he?"

"It seems too soon," said Logan.

"Well," said Cliff. "We miss payments here and there. But we always make them up. We've gotten notices before but we usually pay the late amount on time. Or only a little late. But, yeah, we received a redemption order in the mail a few months ago but we were planning on paying it off."

Logan screwed up his mouth while he contemplated the predicament and then took another bite of his sandwich. Cliff shoved the last of his sandwich in his mouth and stored it in his cheek as he chewed.

"I don't care about this house anymore anyway," Cliff continued. "But it's eating me up not knowing who did it. Was it because of me? Did someone kill Brooke because of me? Did it follow me back from Afghanistan? Wherever I go, the people around me —"

The words trailed off. He walked over to the wall and levered a knife out of it.

"You want to huck some knives?"

"I know this must be insanely hard for you," said Logan. "And you've been through more than most people. But you're balling everything up until it's this enormous thing you can't deal with. What happened to Brooke was different. I think you need to deal with one thing at a time. Break it down into pieces. But I'm good, I'll leave the knife throwing to you."

Clifford stared off into somewhere in the wall. Maybe he was thinking about it. Or maybe he didn't hear a word Logan said.

He flung the knife and it spun in the air until it chunked into the drywall. He walked over, wrested it free. He backed up further away and flung it again. Each time drywall dust crumbled from the other holes punctured in the wall. He repeated this a couple more times before dropping down onto the cigarette-burned recliner.

He pulled out a little jar with a crispy amber-coloured flakes, like the surface of a creme brulee.

"You should smoke some shatter with me and huck some knives," he said.

"I'm good," said Logan.

Clifford broke off a small piece and put it in a thin glass pipe and smoked it. White smoke shot up the shaft of the pipe into Clifford's face. His eyes glazed over and he watched at memories play themselves out in front of him.

"You still with me?" asked Logan.

Clifford nodded slowly while his eyes went through warp drive.

"Why, man?" said Clifford. "Why all of this?"

His shoulders heaved up and down as his breaths got shorter and faster. Tears welled up in his eyes. Then a rage filled his face. A red hot righteous anger.

"They're coming for me too," said Clifford.

Logan leaned forward and tried to catch Clifford's eye.

"Are you sure?" he asked. "How do you know?"

Clifford's jaw shifted from side to side as he ground his teeth.

"I can feel it," he said.

Logan coughed from the secondhand smoke. He knelt up and placed a hand on the coffee table to steady himself.

"Hey," said Logan. "There's a list. Brooke was on it."

Clifford only nodded slightly.

"You know what I mean?"

Cliff closed his eyes tight and opened them again wide like he was driving on the highway and losing focus. His pupils still stared off into somewhere beyond the floor.

"I found a list. Lots of people on it. It's for douchebags and busy-bodies to keep track of everyone."

Cliff's attention stayed somewhere beyond the floor.

"Yo, was Brooke ever married?"

"Yeah," said Clifford. "She was married to a guy named Eugene. They got divorced."

"Do you think Eugene would want to hurt her?"

Clifford looked blankly into the floor.

"No," he said.

"No?" asked Logan. "You don't think he's angry about the divorce?"

"Eugene died three or four years ago," said Cliff.

His gaze stayed on the carpet.

"Heart attack," he noted.

"Do you know about this list Brooke was on?"

"What list?" asked Clifford.

Logan took a deep breath.

"There's a list. On the internet. Some people have access to it and they share information about everybody else," said Logan. "Eugene dragged Brooke pretty hard on it."

"What did he say?"

"That she was mentally unwell and took his hard-earned money," said Logan.

"They had a messy divorce, and her lawyer argued for half or thereabouts," said Cliff. "I only met her after all that happened. It was none of my business so I didn't ask too much about it and she didn't talk about it too much. I know he was an asshole though and treated her bad. Can you show me this list?"

"I don't have access to it," said Logan. "Someone only showed it to me this morning. I don't know if I'll get to see it again."

"Am I on the list?" asked Clifford.

"I didn't have time to look."

"I need to look at this list," said Clifford. "Who showed it to you?"

"A girl I went out with," said Logan.

"Can you take me to her?" asked Clifford.

"I can't do that," said Logan. "She didn't want to show me the list in the first place and I don't think I'm getting a second look. I doubt she'll even answer the phone if I call."

"You must have been some date. Who else has the list?"

"I don't know," said Logan.

"Hold on," said Cliff. "Who is this person you went out with?"

"She's a local mover and shaker," said Logan. "She's an executive for a convention they run in town for New Age health nut types. I was asking her questions and we had a few drinks and went out."

"And she has a list? How many people are on the list?"

"Countless. I couldn't start to guess."

"Why does she have access to the list?"

"I think it's mostly for yuppies and hipsters and rich people, I guess? I don't know. She's on the We Believe in 118 committee. They're trying to improve the neighbourhood, and she said it's important they keep track of the people who live here. But it was also like her personal form of entertainment. But it's not just them. There's no telling how many people subscribe to this list, or how many other lists are out there."

"And Eugene wrote about Brooke on it?"

"Yeah, he made her sound like the worst person ever."

Cliff shook his head.

"Figures. Are you on it?"

"Yeah. It's awful. It's like everyone I've ever met made a record of every mistake I've ever made. All my worst qualities. And exaggerate them for their own entertainment."

"Like what?"

"Like I enjoy an occasional game of cards and some other stuff. Forget about it."

"And we don't know anyone else who has access to this list?"

"Not that I know of. It's hard to tell."

"We must know someone," said Cliff, getting louder.

"There's no saying the list has anything to do with Brooke's murder," said Logan.

"It's too weird though," said Cliff. He stood up and paced back and forth. "I have to know more about this list."

"I don't know, man. Talia's not going to tell us shit. She didn't want to show it to me in the first place."

"We have to find someone else with the list."

"How?"

"Ask people," said Cliff. "Phone this Talia chick. For me."

Clifford paced back and forth, dialing numbers into his phone. Eventually someone on the other end picked up. Cliff asked them if they knew about the list. It sounded as though they didn't know what he was talking about. He hung up and dialed another number. He got an answering machine and he left a broken and breathless message asking if they knew anything about a list that everybody's on. He hung up and dialed another number. Someone picked up. He got angrier and desperate and asked if they knew anything about a list. The person said they didn't know what he was talking about. He ended the call and swore loudly.

He dialed another number.

"Maybe you should take it easy for a bit," said Logan. "We can come up with a plan."

"How else are we going to find it?" said Clifford, his face tight and determined. "Phone her."

He snapped his fingers at Logan. Logan pulled out his phone and called Talia and the call ended abruptly before a single ring.

"She has me blocked," said Logan.

"Call some more people," said Cliff, his phone to his ear.

Logan called Clare.

"Hey. Do you know anything about a list people are on?" asked Logan when she picked up. "A list people subscribe to and share notes on everyone else?"

"What?" she asked. "What are you talking about?"

"A spreadsheet on the internet. People write down notes and gossip about everybody else. People's histories. I'm on it. It says to not hire me for any jobs."

"Logan?" she asked. She sounded sleepy and confused and exasperated. "What? You're not getting a job because of what list?"

"Is Ricky there?" asked Logan. "Can you ask him?"

"Ask him what? About a list? Here, you talk to him," she said and Logan heard her passing the phone over to him.

"Yeah?"

"Ricky, do you know anything about a list people use to keep track of everyone else?"

"What list?" he asked. "The pawn database?"

"No," said Logan. "There's a list on the internet. People subscribe to it and write notes and gossip about everyone else. Do you know this list?"

"I have no idea what you're talking about," said Ricky. "Where are you getting this from?"

"Kenny's neighbour showed it to me," said Logan.

"Does this have something to do with the Corvette?" asked Ricky.

"I'm not sure," said Logan.

Logan tried to describe the list the way he saw it when he was with Talia. Ricky didn't know what Logan was talking about. The conversation fizzled out and Ricky said he had to go.

Clifford was in the kitchen screaming into his phone.

"A list! A list! Everyone's on it. A list! What don't you understand about a list?"

He hung up and growled.

"Cliff, take it easy."

"I'm not going to take it easy," said Cliff. He stormed out the front door and slammed it behind him. Logan chased after him and caught up with him in the front yard.

"Cliff, stop."

Cliff stood breathing heavily and clenching his fists.

"I think I'm on the list," he said.

"So first of all," said Logan. "This list is just a list. We don't know it has anything to do with anything. Why don't we park it to the side as its own thing for now?"

Cliff punched the smiling photo of Darcy Hannigan on the 'For Sale' sign and it made creaking sound as it swung back and forth. A woman pushing a baby carriage crossed the street away from them.

"Let's go inside and think about what we can do."

Cliff's arms dropped by his sides and his chin hit his chest. He growled like an animal. He punched the smiling face of Darcy Hannigan on the 'For Sale' sign again and the sign swung back and forth.

"Come on. Let's go inside."

Cliff swayed a little like he might pick up speed in any direction and eventually he swayed in the right direction back toward the front door of the house. They went back inside. Cliff collapsed back onto the recliner and slumped down so his head was close to his knees. Logan sat back down on the blanket covered couch underneath the wall of knife holes.

"I killed a kid," said Cliff. "In Afghanistan. He was maybe sixteen? He was driving a van straight at a group of our guys who just came out from clearing a house. I shot him. Was he trying to hurt anyone? I don't know."

Cliff kept his eyes shut tight.

"Listen to me," said Logan. "That's serious and I'm sure you did the right thing in the moment. And you should talk to someone about that. A professional."

Cliff nodded without opening his eyes. His hands balled into fists, clenching and releasing and clenching again.

"Take some deep breaths," said Logan. "That was a long time ago."

"It followed me here," said Cliff.

"What did?"

"The war. The war don't stop because you're on the other side of some imaginary border or they're not recognized as state soldiers. There's only the war and that's it."

"You're balling everything up again, man," said Logan. "Let's take it apart, piece by piece."

"Once you understand war, you understand that's all there is. War doesn't keep to itself behind certain borders and not others. War doesn't stay between state sanctioned soldiers on one side against state sanctioned soldiers on the other. It's like a storm. Lots of storms everywhere. Some people are on the inside and some people are on the edge of it. And it moves around. People see it in the news and think it doesn't apply to them. But anybody who gets it, prepares for the storm."

Cliff froze. Logan could see something playing in Cliff's mind right at the front of his forehead.

And then it was gone.

"My buddy was a drone pilot," Cliff said. "He sat in a cock pit in Arizona and piloted drones in the Middle East. Killed people. Didn't know who they were. Kids. Adults. You have no idea. Once they're on the other side of some heat map, it's just like a video game. They're non-entities. On the surface, you don't give a fuck. But then you can't sleep. Get anxiety. Start falling apart. He got a divorce. Only sees his kids with supervision. He's all fucked up now. From fighting the war practically from his bedroom. You ask me what war, what am I supposed to tell you? Between what political and legal parameters would you like me to couch it for you? If I named a country, would that help? Yemen. There you go. This country or that country. The war. The war against everyone."

He shook his head to get something out of his mind. Logan tried to catch his eye again.

"I think when we experience trauma, we get anxiety," said Logan. "And when we get anxiety everything gets built up into one big knot and it gets overwhelming. You need to dismantle this war in your mind into its separate components."

"I need to get out of here," said Cliff.

"Where?"

Cliff shot up and jumped into his bedroom. He pulled a large duffel bag out of the closet and shoved clothes into it.

"I've been so fucking stupid," said Cliff. He pulled more clothes off hooks in the closet and shoved them into the bag.

"What's going on?" asked Logan.

"I've just been sitting here, waiting for them to come back for me," he said. "So stupid."

"Waiting for who?"

"They're going to come back for me," he said. "I've been an idiot to sit here waiting for them."

"For who?"

"For the people who killed Brooke," he said. "They're going to come back and finished the job. I need to get out of here."

"This isn't the war, Cliff."

"Then what is it?"

"It's not terrorists from Afghanistan."

"What's the difference?"

He stomped into the bathroom and grabbed some toiletries and shoved them into the duffel bag. He picked up his keys.

"Call me if you learn anything else about this list."

"Where are you going?"

"I'm going to sleep in my truck for a while. Maybe head out to the bush."

He strode out the front door and left it swinging wide open. Logan listened to him start up his pickup truck and rumble away.

Logan picked up the last of his sandwich and took a bite out of it. He stood in the centre of the room and listened to the silence now all the energy had flown out the door. Logan left and closed the door behind him and finished his sandwich as he walked up the street to the bus stop. He took the bus back to his apartment and lugged his way up the stairs.

He sat on his dining chair at the table and shuffled cards and thought about his conversation with Cliff. When he wanted a break from shuffling, he lay on the couch and looked up at the ceiling and pondered the nature of Cliff's problems. Then after a while he got up and resumed practicing blind riffles and cuts that appear like a thorough shuffle but actually maintain the deck in its intended order.

He repeated this back-and-forth from the table to the couch until it got dark and then he eased himself into bed with Cliff's words still echoing in his mind. They bounced around in Logan's skull as he fell asleep.

And when he woke up the next morning, he knew who killed Kenny Prince and took the Corvette.

18

Every year, one in a hundred people are the victim of a violent crime. Police solve about 63 percent of them. Of those that are homicides, the close rate is a bit better - 70 percent. But still, about 30 percent of homicides go unsolved.

Cars are tougher. Only 13 percent of vehicle thefts are solved by police. That is to say, resulting in convictions of the guy who took it. And of those stolen cars themselves, one in four disappear off the face of the earth forever. Poof. Gone.

They're very different crimes. To solve a homicide, you look at the family and people closest to the victim. You look at the time of death and the manner in which they were killed. You determine the location of the murder and the body. These things start filling in a picture.

But applying this methodology to a stolen car doesn't get you anywhere. Vehicle theft doesn't work like a homicide. Vehicle theft is a numbers game.

The numbers tell us what cars are most likely stolen. They tell us where they are most likely stolen from and where those stolen cars most likely go. And as opposed to homicide, it's usually not perpetrated by a family member or a friend. It's usually committed by a stranger.

The police were trying to solve Kenny Prince's murder as a homicide when they should have been trying to solve it like a vehicle theft.

Logan thought about it more sideways.

When Logan tried to think about the murder of Kenny Prince, the faces of the people he met got in the way. Kenny's daughter Valerie. Dennis at the RV park. Talia. When he closed his eyes, their faces felt so close he could touch them. He could perceive the pores in their skin and the tiny little hairs around their ears. It felt like they were trying to tell him something but the words they spoke were ambient and formless.

It wasn't until Logan concentrated on the car that he could let their faces fade away. He let go of their faces, and their homes, and he let go of himself and his own apartment.

He let go of everything until there were only the numbers running everything underneath. He thought about the odds.

The odds Kenny Prince and Brooke Esterly were killed by a stranger - 3:1.

The odds Kenny Prince's murderer took the car - 2:1.

The odds the killer sold it to a chop shop - 4:1.

If the killer sold it to a chop shop, the odds the killer is connected to organized crime - 2:1.

The odds the killer is hiding the car - 6:1.

If the killer is hiding the car, then the odds the killer owns a garage or some kind of Quonset - 2:1.

If the killer took the Corvette, the odds they live within a 50 mile radius - 4:1.

If the killer lives in a 50 mile radius, then the odds they live within the city limits - 3:1.

He could feel the odds rise up in the form of waves around him — endless series of probabilities floating up and down.

Logan's heart rate accelerated as the waves of numbers seemed to lift him out of his bed and into the air. He was adrift on a sea of odds and he hovered, exhilarated and scared, and felt the numbers flowing through every person and every thing. His fingertips buzzed with the sensation of the numbers flowing through them.

He could feel the likelihood of the neighbour being in a car crash (366:1). If they are in a car crash, the odds of them dying (100:1). He could feel the odds of someone burglarizing an apartment in his building (36:1). The odds of dying from an injury (17:1).

Everything clicked and lined up for him according to a range of odds. He was riding a numbers wave.

"It's like a video game," Cliff had said back at his house. Those words bounced around inside Logan's skull all night.

There was a distance between Cliff's buddy who piloted drones from Arizona and the people he killed in Afghanistan. It felt the same as the distance between the list and the people described on it, like the virtual separation a video game provides from real life.

The ocean of numbers rose up and presented Kenny Prince's killer and then gently put Logan back down on his bed.

He unplugged the phone from the charger on the wall and pulled up the odds-on favourite to be Kenny and Brooke's murderer.

The 420 Xanax Mafia.

When BB had shown their social media posts to Logan in his car, they seemed like punk kids. Punk kids with a lot of Xanax and time on their hands, but punk kids all the same. But there was a distance between them and whatever social media reality they were trying to connect with. That same kind of distance between Cliff's buddy piloting drones in Arizona and the people he was killing in Afghanistan that made it feel like a video game. The same distance between the people taking notes on a list on the internet and the people they described. To the degree the internet brought the world together, it separated people so much further away.

Logan tapped the #420xanaxmafia hashtag and scrolled through a series of photos. Most of the photos with the #420xanaxmafia hashtag showed young men. Teenagers, mostly. Caucasian. They posed like they were on the covers of rap albums but they were skinny, and a softness around the jowls betrayed their suburban upbringing.

Many of the kids wore golf visors on their foreheads with spiked blond hair poking out over top. They almost always wore expensive looking sunglasses. They wore jeans or basketball shorts.

They often posed with large stacks of money. One kid held four ribbon-wrapped bundles of bills up over his shoulders like they were dumbbells as he posed in his bedroom.

Another kid showed a bowl full of Xanax pills next to a gaming computer lit up like the Empire State Building whenever the Yankees won a division.

Another photo showed a laundry room with a kid wearing some kind of ninja costume like a cosplay, with a black mask over his mouth and he posed with a couple handguns under a poster of Al Pacino's Scarface above the laundry hamper full of clothes.

Below that someone posted a crude music video of a home-recorded rap song. Logan tapped the play button and a tinny beat rattled in the background as synth noises washed over top. The kid mumbled something about a girl not loving him and how the drugs helped to dull the anger. He gestured awkwardly as he rapped, trying to act like a rap mogul but he looked more like a frustrated hospital patient asking for something he couldn't express.

One kid posed with a couple bikini-clad women next to a pool in Vegas. The women were twice his age. Another kid drove a Lamborghini in Miami. Another kid smoked a cannon of a joint on a rooftop in New York.

While it wasn't a certainty one of these kids killed Kenny Prince and took the Corvette, the numbers surged through Logan's fingertips and almost tapped the links for him. It was like holding a pair of aces. It wasn't a guaranteed hit but something outside himself pushed him onward.

He thumbed through the series of selfies of money and drugs and vacation shots and video game clips and landed at one in particular. It was fairly unremarkable compared to the others. But it spoke to him.

The kid wore a bandanna over his mouth and crouched next to a Rottweiler in the front yard. His username was CoDPimp. There weren't any other houses along the street behind him, only orange sticks poking out of the ground in empty mud lots to indicate underground powerlines. The setting sun created long shadows from the sticks that stretched out ten feet or so into the street. The sky was mostly clear but a couple hazy clouds glowed a dusky shade of orange.

It looked like an Edmonton sky. A hazy kind of tangerine overhead that felt more local than anywhere else in the world.

Logan sent CoDPimp a message.

"I'm looking for a Corvette. If you know the one, leave it for me in the parking lot of the Northgate Wal-Mart on 97th. Your business is your business. I don't care. I just need the car. I imagine you don't need the attention."

Logan stood up and paced in his room, the numbers still buzzing through his body to the tips of his fingers. He needed to hit a casino while the numbers surged through him, practically lining up to do his bidding, but it was five o'clock in the morning and The Money Store didn't open until nine.

Logan put on coffee and shuffled cards while he waited. As he shucked the cards over and over in his hands, he grew increasingly haunted by the list Talia showed him. How many people accessed the list? What did the people close to him know about him? He didn't know who knew what sordid details about him and whether he was destined to spend the rest of his life being manipulated by the kind of people who would bullwhip him in the street if they thought it would get them one rung higher on the corporate ladder.

If there was one list people subscribed to, it stood to reason there were more lists out there. Lists shared between gangsters, lists shared between human resources and staffing companies, friends and family, thieves and political parties, Masons and Mansons, and new flings and old flames. There was no way of knowing who accessed these lists and there was no way of knowing what people wrote about Logan on them. What enemies had Logan made along the way, and what might they want others to think about Logan? The thought of people like Talia playing him for a fool made him whip the cards down to the table harder. They riffled with a slapping sound louder and louder the more he thought about it.

Nine o'clock eventually dragged its way to the present. Logan grabbed his jacket and left the apartment.

His neighbour Nia was getting home with several bags of groceries. Logan said hello as he passed by.

"Hi, Logan," she said, smiling into her door as though something was terribly funny. Or awkward. She avoided eye contact as though there was something excruciating about looking at Logan's face. Logan paused to look back at her and she kept smiling as she disappeared into her apartment.

Logan made his way downstairs.

People milled about the avenue. Logan hunched his shoulders up by his ears as he walked and kept his eyes on the sidewalk, avoiding the moment in someone's eyes when they might recognize him and quickly look away.

He pulled out the phone and called Ricky.

"Yo, did you see I got that Civic?"

"What the hell happened to it? You roll it off the highway?"

"The fucker came at us with a baseball bat. He smashed the hell out of it as I was driving away."

"Us? What do you mean 'us?'"

"Me. The royal 'we'. Me and the car."

"Christ," said Ricky. "Yeah I can give you some money but I'm out of town right now. I'm in Wetaskiwin. A guy wants to sell me a couple palettes of work clothes. Come by Monday."

"Alright," said Logan and he hung up.

All the way down the sidewalk people seemed to look him up and down or scrutinize him out of the sides of their eyes.

He scurried his way down the few blocks to The Money Store and stood in line. At the front of the store, a waxen-faced woman behind bulletproof glass took people's papers in a revolving metal dish in the counter. The fluorescent lights throbbed against the bright orange walls.

The guy at the window couldn't provide pay stubs and tried arguing his case.

"I do home repairs," he pleaded. "I'm self-employed."

The woman's face morphed into a blank wall as she explained she'd need his past two years of tax records. The guy spun around and left cursing as he pushed his way out the door.

The next guy in line carried a hard hat and wore muddy work boots and seemed to have fewer problems. She took his papers and told him to have a seat. She rolled herself on her office chair around a corner and after a few minutes rolled herself back to the window. The construction worker approached the counter and she counted out money into the metal dish and spun it around to him. He snatched it up, shoved it in his wallet and walked out the door.

Logan stepped up to the window. She sighed.

"Hi, Logan," she said with a dour note in her voice.

"Hoping I can get a top-up," he said.

"Your details still the same? Same employer?"

Logan nodded.

"Let me check," she said. She adjusted the position of the laptop mounted on a swivel stand and typed into it. Logan watched her eyes flick back and forth as she read.

"You're behind on a couple payments," she said. "I can do a hundred and forty dollars."

"That's not enough," said Logan. "I've paid in thousands of dollars to this place. You know I'm good for it."

"That's all I'm approved for," she said. "My hands are tied. Take it or leave it."

"Fine," said Logan. He signed the paperwork and she spun a hundred and forty dollars around in the little metal dish.

He grabbed the money and as he turned around she said, "Make good choices."

Logan turned back around.

"Why wouldn't I make good choices?"

"I didn't mean nothing," she said. "I was just saying 'don't gamble it all away' or something."

"Why would you think I'd gamble it away?" said Logan.

"We get lots of gamblers in here," she said. "I don't care what you do with it."

Logan opened his mouth to say something but shut it and walked out.

A young couple walked by him. They carried tall cups of coffee and shopping bags, and when they came close to Logan they both turned their heads to look away. Logan tried to make eye contact. Were they avoiding him on purpose? Or were they just not looking at him?

His phone vibrated in his pocket. It was a response from CoDPimp. It read: "Fuck off."

19

Logan could still feel the numbers buzzing through his fingers and needed to make use of them before they drifted away. He threw himself onto the 114 bus and while it lurched along the road Logan sent another message to CoDPimp.

It read: "Up to you. Just leave the car at the Northgate Wal-Mart or we can do this the way that involves police."

Before the end of the ride a little check mark noted the message as read but no response came. Logan stepped off the bus outside the large shining doors of Millenium Casino. Two spotlights on either side of the doors remained off, pointed heavenward and collecting dust and cobwebs until the next aging rock star passed through their venue. Logan threaded his way through the VLTs to the cage. He dug the money out of his pocket and a woman with a feathery 1980s hairdo handed him a tray of poker chips. He hustled over to the poker room at the back and landed at a Hold 'Em table with a mixed assortment of very single-looking men. Divorced guys leaned back with smug looks on their faces. Nerdy looking younger men in ball caps and sunglasses hovered around looking like they had a bigger interest in poker ranges than getting laid.

And at the moment Logan sat down, the number wave that had surrounded him and lifted him up and surged through his veins now all of a sudden drifted away, faded into the floor, faded into nothingness. The blood drained out of his face as the blinds whittled away at his small stack of chips. Tens and Jacks floated into his hands to taunt him all the way down.

A guy who looked like Santa Claus sat next to Logan and exchanged knowing glances with another guy at the table. He had a white beard, a wool coat with big black boots and a big black belt.

Logan tried to raise on another Jack-Ten and promptly lost it. He threw his cards down in exasperation.

"Someone's going to go cry in the bathroom," said the Santa Claus-looking guy.

"Who are you?" said Logan.

"Nobody," said the Santa Claus guy.

Logan sneered at him.

"I'd say you look like a nobody," said Logan.

Santa Claus guffawed at Logan. Logan leaned in to Santa Claus' ear.

"You ever had your teeth smashed out on a poker table, Nobody?" whispered Logan.

Santa Claus shoved Logan's shoulder. Logan jumped out of his seat. Santa stood up to square off with Logan.

"Santa Claus-looking motherfucker."

Logan went in swinging. Santa Claus was able to swat away a couple of his punches but Logan managed to land a decent one on Santa Claus' chin before security marched over and twisted Logan's arm behind his back.

"Take your chips," one of the security guys said.

Logan grabbed his remaining chips with his right hand and shoved them in his pocket. Then the security guards steered Logan into a little holding cell with sheet metal walls. They threw him down onto the floor of the cell where he looked back between the legs of one of the security guys at the door they came in from and then looked ahead at another plain door on the other side of the cell.

They kicked Logan around. One put Logan in a full-Nelson while the other slugged Logan in the stomach. It knocked the wind out of him and then the first guy pounded the side of his head a couple times. Then they opened the other door on the other end of the cell and ejected Logan into the back alley where he landed in a mud puddle behind the kitchen grease bin.

"You're barred for two weeks, Logan," one of the security guards said and they turned their backs and wandered off behind the back door.

A couple line cooks stood by the kitchen loading door and gawked at Logan as they puffed on their vapes. He propped himself up on his hands and knees and opened and closed his eyes a few times while the world wobbled around him. He crouched again on his forearms and let his head sag a while and concentrated on breathing. Eventually he crawled over to the dumpster and pulled himself up along the side and leaned his back against it.

He pulled out his phone and called Clare.

A light rain misted the air by the time Clare pulled up and found him sitting on the ground at the edge of the parking lot, slumped under a lamp post. He was still, and his hair and jacket damp.

Clare couldn't look at him and stared straight ahead as he climbed in the passenger side.

Neither said anything as she pulled out of the parking lot and along the service road that connected to the main street.

"Thanks," said Logan.

She shook her head.

She gestured with her hand, her fingers shooting forward as she made pointed remarks in her mind, going over what she wanted to say, her tongue in a constant state of being held. Until she let it go.

"What the fuck are you doing?"

"I'm sorry," said Logan.

"Like, seriously, what the fuck are you doing? I can't do this anymore, Logan. Can you just go one week without being a fuck up?"

"The other guy started it," said Logan.

"Other people always seem to be starting with you, Logan. Other people start it with you more than anyone I know and the result is always the same. You've gambled all your money away, you're laying beaten up in some puddle, and you absolutely refuse to care about yourself or me. When are you going to get your shit together?"

"Right now. I'm done with all this shit," said Logan. "I just want to be on my feet properly. No more gambling. No more fighting. Start fixing my place up. Make it comfier for people. Own things."

"I don't believe you," she said.

"I am. I promise."

"I'm tired of the promises. I'm sorry. I just don't believe you. I'd like to but I don't anymore. Before, I could trick myself into believing you. Or tell myself I believed you even when I knew I didn't. But now I don't even have the energy for that anymore. I just don't believe you."

"I understand. I'll just have to show you. It'll be different —"

"I'm at the point where maybe I have to cut you off. This is affecting me too, Logan. It's hurting me. Maybe you need to not have someone there for you in order to change, or maybe you won't. Maybe one of these days you're going to get seriously hurt. Or you're going to be homeless again. But I have to protect myself Logan. It's gets too hard on me. I have to look after me too."

"I understand."

"I don't think you do."

She cried silently the rest of the way to Logan's apartment building. Logan kept his mouth shut. They listened to the car splash through the thin layer of rain on the street and the wipers rub against the windshield until they arrived at his front door.

"Thanks," said Logan as he got out of the car. "I appreciate it."

Clare looked away out the driver's side window and said nothing as he shut the door.

20

Logan spent most of the night shuffling cards. By the next morning, the fading on the backs of the cards swelled into large white spots. The edges showed fraying and creases along the corners. They lost their snap and a certain bounce in his fingertips. He needed a new deck of cards. A proper deck. Not the plastic window scrapers from the dollar store. Logan paced until the sun came up, wringing his hands and shaking his head at himself. Once the sun was up, he grabbed his jacket and walked to the bus stop.

When he got there, the bus shelter was crowded and everyone seemed to be looking at him. He slipped in between people who looked him up and down. He glared back.

The number 9 bus pulled up and Logan sat down on the seat behind the back door and plexi-glass parition. A man in a dark suit sat next to him.

The bus pulled away. Logan rested his head against the window and listened to the crunch of the wheels over gravel and the rattle of the engine. They crossed the Yellowhead and went under a bridge with train cars parked above and the bus' brakes whined as it approached a bus stop.

The man in the dark suit next to Logan turned to him and said, "Drop the Corvette. Forget about it."

"What?" said Logan. He tried to focus on the man's face but the man turned away slightly. He wore sunglasses. Clean hair cut. Dark hair. Indistinct features.

"It's just a car. Forget about it. Move on with your life."

The man stood up and walked toward the back door as the bus pulled up to the platform. Logan stood up.

"Who are you?" asked Logan through the plexi-glass.

The man pushed his way between some other passengers and then he was gone, out the door, and lost in the parking lot outside.

The door closed and the bus pulled away. Logan sat back down and wondered if what just took place had really happened.

Logan pushed his way out through the throng of people entering the bus at the Northgate platform.

Some working stiff grumbled as Logan squeezed past him.

"Get the fuck out of my way," said Logan.

"Fuck you."

"Fuck you."

A bitter wind blew in carrying the smell of coming winter. Logan hustled his way through the crowd of people on the bus platform and across the street to the Wal-Mart. He walked up one lane of parking stalls and down another looking for the Corvette. The lot was full. Vehicles jockeyed for position for open spaces. Logan walked up another lane and down another, burying his chin in his chest as he braced against the cold.

A pickup truck honked at Logan. He looked inside. Some guy in a baseball cap and sunglasses with his girlfriend in the passenger seat slowed down. The driver gave Logan the middle finger while his girlfriend laughed.

"Pile of trash," the driver called out at Logan.

Did they know Logan? From the list perhaps? There was no way to know.

Logan gestured with both hands for the guy to get out and square up but the truck simply sped off. Logan patrolled the parking lot, up and down every lane. The Corvette didn't present itself, and after Logan had walked down the last lane of parked cars he stepped into the mall attached behind the Wal-Mart.

Most of the stalls were closed down. The upstairs was taken up by medical and dental offices.

On the main floor, the surviving units were taken up by a barber, a tobacconist, and a place called Discount Jewelry.

An electronic chime sounded as Logan walked into Capitol Games, the little gaming shop wedged between a defunct ex-aquarium store and a cannabis paraphernalia shop at the end of a darkened hall. Board games filled the shelves at the front of the store. A couple pool tables, a poker table, and some sort of shuffleboard table took up the back. Dart boards lined the walls.

"Logan," said Telly behind the counter. "Not playing with a full deck or what?"

Telly was a squat, balding man who spent his whole life in the store, usually with a phone under each ear as he haggled over the prices of rare Magic: The Gathering cards.

"What?" asked Logan.

"I said, 'You not playing with a full deck anymore or what?'"

"What do you mean by that?" asked Logan.

"I'm joking," he said. "You getting a pack of cards? Or anything else I can help you with?"

"Pack of Bee," said Logan, reaching for his wallet.

"Limited edition chrome?"

"Classic."

"Red or blue?"

"Whatever. Blue."

Telly pulled out the pack from a tray behind him and plopped it down on the counter.

"Four-fifty," he said.

Logan dug out the change from his wallet.

"Want to see a trick?" asked Telly.

"Alright."

Telly pulled a deck of cards out from the till. A pack of Bicycle with blue backs. He shuffled them with a few swift stock shuffles and a couple riffles. Then he handed them to Logan.

"Shuffle those. Inspect them. Whatever."

Logan riffled them a couple times, fanned them out to make sure they were a regular deck of cards. Then he squared them in his hands to double check the size and that there were no irregular edges. Then he put the deck on the counter.

Telly fanned the cards out and told Logan to pick one. Logan pulled out an Eight of Clubs and slid it back into the fanned out cards.

Telly shuffled the cards again with a couple drop shuffles and a couple quick riffles. He put the deck down and flipped the top card over onto the counter. A Jack of Diamonds.

"This is the story of a guy named Jack," said Telly. "And the King of Egypt told him he needed to find the lost treasure of Egypt."

He flipped over a King of Spades off the top of the deck as he spoke. Then he pulled out all four Fours from the deck and placed them next to each other, face up.

"So he traveled to the four corners of the Earth and spoke with three queens."

He produced the Queen of Spades from the top of the deck.

"He spoke to the Queen of Spades and asked where he could find the lost treasure of Egypt. She said it was not his to find for he was not worthy."

He shuffled the cards and then a light flourish, the Queen of Clubs flipped off the top of the deck and he placed it next to the first queen.

"So he spoke to the Queen of Clubs and asked where he could find the lost treasure of Egypt. She said the path to the treasure was too perilous and no one would ever find it. He would certainly be eaten alive by demons."

Telly gave the cards another quick shuffle and placed them down in the counter.

With another light touch, the Queen of Hearts seemed to jump by itself from the top of the deck.

"Finally he talked to the Queen of Hearts, and she said to abandon his quest because the King of Hearts was watching and would certainly have him killed if he got too close."

"But Jack kept on looking. After many defeats he began to think perhaps it was true that he was not worthy. Then he was plagued by terrible demons — his own demons from within. But he dug deep and eventually he was able to overcome them. And it was then he knew where the treasure was and he raced to tell the King of Spades and an agent of the King of Hearts came to kill Jack and Jack defeated him too.

"It was only after he looked inside himself and decided he was worthy, and he defeated those demons from within, and defeated all the king's men that he could unlock the location of the lost treasure of Egypt. It was in Egypt all the time, hidden in plain sight. Only those who decide themselves worthy and can defeat those demons are able to see it. Then the treasure becomes apparent to them. And it's so beautiful you can't not see it."

He pulled out a Joker.

"Is this your card?"

"No," said Logan.

"Oh," said Telly, looking disappointed. He placed the Joker on the counter face up. "Well, how about this one? Is this your card?" He slid out another Joker. Logan smiled.

"Nope," said Logan.

"Hmmm," said Telly with a mock perplexed look on his face. He put the other Joker down next to the first one.

"Well it's got to be around here somewhere."

Telly spread the cards out on the counter, face down in one long arc. Along the row of blue cards, a red card stuck out like a red neon light. Telly pretended not to notice it.

"I'll see if I can pick up on its vibrations."

Telly hovered his hands over the cards pretending to feel for their vibrations and ignored the obvious red card. Finally, his hands stopped over the red card.

"Oh," he said. "Here. I feel something around here."

Logan smiled and shook his head.

Telly pulled the red card out and flipped it up to Logan. It was his Eight of Clubs.

"Is this your card?"

Logan laughed.

"That was a good one."

Logan stared down at the cards and leaned in over the counter.

"Have you heard anything about me?" he asked, almost whispering.

"What do you mean?"

"What do you know about me?"

"Nothing, man," said Telly, taking a step back.

"For sure," said Logan. "Sorry. Forget it. Someone's going around saying stuff about me."

"Don't let the bastards drag you down, man" said the guy. "Take it easy."

"Have a good day," said Logan, and left the store.

Logan muttered to himself all the way back to the Northgate bus platform. He got on the bus and looked for the man in the dark suit but he never appeared.

When he got back to his apartment, he locked the door and sat down at the dinner table. He pushed his old deck of cards to one side and unwrapped the new deck of cards, and resumed shuffling. He focused on shuffling the cards at an even rhythm. His hands shook and his leg jittered under the table. He tried to breathe through it. Top card to second position, then to third, then to fourth, and then back up to the top.

And then back to two. Riffle. Square. To three. Riffle. Square. To four. Riffle. Square.

There was a knock at the door.

"Hello?"

It was quiet. Then they knocked again.

"Hello?"

Logan got up and opened the door. A young man with a bandanna over his nose and mouth and ski goggles over his eyes stood in the hallway holding a broadsword.

"What the fuck?" said Logan.

The kid swung the sword at Logan's head. Logan flopped backward onto the floor and the sword cleaved into the door frame above him.

21

Logan lay frozen on his back and looked up at the kid wrestling the sword out of the door frame. His brown hair spiked out from the ski goggles for a pointy crown effect, like he was some kind of key chain troll doll.

"Who are you?" asked Logan.

The kid paid no attention as he put his foot against the door frame and wrested the blade out of the wood.

"What the hell?" asked Logan.

Logan crab-walked backward as best he could and gained about a foot of distance.

The kid heaved the sword up and chopped it down. Logan twisted to his side and the sword cut into the vinyl kitchen floor.

Logan pulled himself up on the counter.

The kid swung again, cutting a gash into the kitchen counter.

"Will you fucking stop?" said Logan, twisting away.

The kid stabbed toward Logan's chest. Logan ran backwards into the living room and the kid intensified his stabs, trying to keep pace as Logan dodged from side to side. They wrestled their way into the dining area. Logan anticipated the kid's lunge as the kid swung across Logan's chest. Logan leaned backward so the sword swung downward in front of him, and then Logan pushed forward and grabbed the kid's throat and pushed him back against the wall.

"Who are you?" Logan asked, squeezing the kid's throat.

Between them, the kid switched his hands on the hilt of the sword and brought it up between them, driving the brass handle into Logan's chin. It forced Logan to lose his grip on the kid's throat. And then the kid got him a second time, which sent Logan staggering backward again. The blow made Logan's eyes well up. The kid kicked Logan's knee, sending him crumpling to the ground.

Through one eye Logan could make out the kid's shape lifting the sword again and Logan crawled under the table. The kid had to change his stance to stab the sword under the table. In that second, Logan came out the other side of the table and he grabbed his dining chair by the legs.

The kid held his sword up by his side and backed into the living room as he sized up what Logan was going to do with the chair. The faded brown chair was light, with foam padding under the polyester fabric, and only hollow metal beams giving it form. Logan drove it straight forward into the kid's stomach. The kid pushed him back and then Logan clubbed him over the head with the chair.

The hollow metal legs were too light to cause significant damage but Logan intensified the blows, faster and faster, whipping the kid over the head repeatedly. It was enough to prevent the kid from taking up a stance with the broadsword.

Again and again, Logan smacked the chair over the kid's head until chair bent out of shape and the polyester ripped. Finally the kid tried to shake him off. It exposed his face long enough for Logan to bat the metal edge of the seat's backrest into the kid's jaw. As the kid tried to roll away from the blow, Logan kicked him in the balls. The kid dropped the sword and fetal positioned on the ground.

While the kid coiled on the floor, Logan tossed the tangled mess of metal rods, polyester and foam to the side. He grabbed duct tape out of the kitchen drawer, knelt down and wrestled the kid's ankles in one arm like a calf-roper and wrapped them up in duct tape.

He straddled the kid and grabbed his arms. The kid resisted but the adrenaline running through Logan allowed him to operate in strong, decisive movements the kid couldn't compete with.

Then he rolled off and rested against the fridge as he caught his breath. The kid said nothing.

Logan looked at his phone trying to decide who to call.

His thumb hovered over Ricky's number but Logan decided against it and put his phone down in his lap again. His hands shook. He took deep breaths.

He picked up the phone again and called Clifford.

"What's up?" asked Cliff.

"I've got a situation," said Logan. He took a second to catch his breath. "Someone tried to kill me. I got him tied up here. I don't know what to do with him."

"Kick the shit out of him," said Cliff.

"I did that."

"Is it the guy who killed Brooke?"

"I don't know if it's him. It's some kid with a sword. Not sure what to do with him now."

"I'm coming over."

Cliff hung up.

The kid groaned and stretched out.

"Fuck you," said Logan.

"I need to use the bathroom," the kid said.

"Seriously?"

"I need to pee."

Logan sighed and looked around the room. Then he grabbed the kid by the armpits and dragged him down the hall into the bathroom. He hoisted the kid onto the edge of the bathtub.

"Can't I piss in the toilet?" the kid said.

Logan pushed him backwards into the bathtub.

"Am I just supposed to piss myself?"

"I don't care," said Logan. "Stay there and be quiet."

Logan went back to the kitchen, leaned against the fridge and slid down to the floor.

The drop in adrenaline made him feel drowsy and he didn't notice the time go by before there was a knock at the door. It was Cliff.

"You got here fast," said Logan.

"Where is he?" he asked.

Logan directed him to the bathroom. Cliff wore army boots and put one up on the edge of the bathtub.

"Do you know who I am?" asked Cliff.

The kid gave no response.

"I'm Brooke's husband," he said.

The kid stayed still.

Cliff prodded the kid with his boot.

"Hey," said Cliff. "Why'd you do it?"

The kid looked away into the wall tiles.

"Hey. I'm talking to you, you little shit," said Cliff, his voice raising in volume. "Did you kill Brooke?"

"I don't know any Brooke," said the kid.

"Who are you?" asked Logan.

The kid stayed quiet.

"I'll let the courts settle this," the kid sneered.

Cliff picked the kid up by the shirt.

"I'm the one who's going to settle this, you little prick," he said, and dropped the kid back in the bathtub.

"You have about two seconds to start telling me who you are and what your fucking story is," said Cliff. "After that we start kicking your teeth out and take it from there."

The kid started kicking at the edge of tub and kicking his feet against the bottom.

"Help!" yelled the kid. "Call the police! Someone call the police!"

Cliff cursed under his breath as he leaned in and popped his fist into the kid's nose. Blood streamed out of it.

"You can cut that out right now," said Cliff.

The kid squirmed in the tub. Blood from his nose smeared against the side of the tub. Urine soaked through the front of his jeans.

"What did you do that for?" moaned the kid.

"Jesus, you are dumb, aren't you?" said Cliff.

"Why did you come to attack me today?" asked Logan.

"Fuck you," said the kid, starting to cry.

"Logan," said Cliff. "Get me a face cloth."

Logan grabbed one from next to the sink.

"Will this work?"

"Perfect."

Cliff wet the face cloth under the bath tap until it was soaked.

The kid squirmed and kicked, anticipating the unpleasantness of what was coming.

Cliff picked him up by the armpits and tried to swing him around in the tub. The kid fell sideways, scrunched in the middle of the tub. He kicked back up at Cliff and balled himself up in the middle of tub.

Cliff popped him a couple more times in the face and then grabbed the kid's feet and spun him around in the tub, pulling his feet up against the back wall. Then he covered the kid's face with the face cloth. He wrapped his hand around the kid's throat and jammed his head under the tap. He turned the tap on and let the water pour over the cloth on the kid's face. The kid started choking.

"Cliff, what are you doing?" asked Logan. "Stop."

Cliff turned the water off.

"Who are you?" asked Cliff. "Who are you?"

The kid spluttered and cried.

Cliff socked the kid in the face again and put his head back under the tap and turned the water back on.

"Cliff, what the fuck," said Logan. "Stop. We can do this another way."

A few seconds went by and then the kid convulsed and coughed up water.

"Tanner," the kid said, coughing up more water. "My name is Tanner."

"What are you doing here, Tanner?" asked Clifford.

"I want to go home," said the kid.

"Wrong answer," said Cliff, turning the water back on. Tanner's body lashed about and he yelled. When he yelled he swallowed water, which sent him choking again. Cliff turned off the water.

"I'm a hit man," said Tanner, after the choking.

"You're a pretty shitty hit man, Tanner," said Cliff. "Who are you a hit man for?"

"No one," he said.

Cliff reached for the tap.

"No, please," said Tanner. "I'll tell you everything. Please let me out of the bathtub. I'll tell you everything. Please."

Cliff looked back at Logan and returned his attention to Tanner. Tanner choked and gasped for air.

"Alright, Tanner," said Cliff. "We're going to leave the washroom now and we're going to talk in the living room like reasonable people. If I don't like your answers, we come straight back to the tub. You understand me?"

The kid nodded. He pulled the kid up and held him by the elbow. Tanner, ankles wrapped in duct tape, hopped down the hall. Once in the living room he dropped down onto the couch. Logan and Cliff stood facing him in the middle of the room.

"Why were you trying to kill me, Tanner?"

"I took a job on you," said the kid.

"Who's paying you?"

"There's no way to know," said the kid. "Your name was on a list."

"Did you kill my wife, Tanner? Did you kill Brooke Esterly?"

The kid shook his head no.

"This was my first job," said Tanner. "Look, I don't know what I'm doing. I'm really sorry. Can you just let me go? I'm just an idiot."

Tanner cried some more.

"We'll see about that Tanner," said Cliff. "First we're going to need more information. How'd you take this job, Tanner?"

"From a list," he said. "On the dark web."

"What list?"

"It doesn't have a name," he said. "It updates itself. The Four-Twenty Xanax Mafia takes jobs off it."

"The Four-Twenty Xanax Mafia," Cliff repeated, slowly, as though to make sure he had heard correctly.

"Who, or what, is the Four-Twenty Xanax Mafia?" asked Logan.

"Nothing," said Tanner. "It's like a club or a gang on the internet. They get paid in crypto. There's a list of names and how much crypto-currency you get for taking someone out. Each name has a link to a printable QR code, so you print it off onto sticker paper. When you get the kill, you put the QR code next to the body, take a photo, and submit it. Once the kill is confirmed, the Bitcoin, Ethereum, FlappyCoin, whatever, gets transferred to your account automatically. Totally anonymous."

"How'd you find out about this list?" asked Cliff.

"No, wait, hold up," said Logan. "How much was the bounty on my name?"

"Point zero five Bitcoin," said Tanner.

"How much is that in regular dollars?"

"About four thousand bucks," said Tanner.

"You were going to kill me for four thousand dollars?" said Logan. He paced back and forth across the apartment. He started fuming and his eyes locked on Tanner's face.

"Let's take him back to the tub," said Logan.

Cliff told Logan to shush and got between him and Tanner.

"How'd you find this list?"

"I don't know," said Tanner. "However people find things on the internet. I search the dark web, I follow people on social media. I check stuff out. These guys aren't even the biggest ones out there. They're kind of low key but the bigger guys involved with it are pretty hardcore."

"What other guys? Who are they?"

"I don't know their names," said Tanner. "You would have to be pretty stupid to put your name out there. But they'll hack social media accounts and show pictures of themselves in Vegas or wherever or just chilling, smoking blunts and playing video games. Whatever. Pictures of cars and parties and stuff."

"And these guys are pretty cool are they?" asked Logan.

"They're gangsters," said Tanner.

"And these guys run a list of people to be killed on the internet?"

"Nobody runs it. Nobody knows who started it," said Tanner. "But anyone can start a list. This one's really deep though. It draws from so many other lists out there. Dozens of them. Maybe hundreds. When people subscribe to lists they pay a fee. That money accumulates in a blockchain account. The list collates all the data from all the other lists and once someone is problematic enough on a bunch of different lists, they get slotted higher on the hit list. The reward for that person goes up as people add negative information about them on their lists. Once someone is worth enough, someone will take the job by clicking the link to print the QR code."

"And you thought that would a pretty reasonable way of conducting your life?"

"You don't look like you have things too figured out yourself," said Tanner.

Logan walked down the hall to his bedroom, unplugged his laptop from the wall and brought it to Tanner.

"Show me," he said.

"This will take a while," said Tanner.

"I don't have any plans," said Logan.

Logan got a knife from the drawer and cut the duct tape off the kid's wrists. The kid tapped away at the laptop, and downloaded a VPN and an encrypted browser. While they waited for the downloads the kid asked for a glass of water. Cliff and Logan looked at each other. Logan went over and grabbed a glass of water for the kid.

After some time, the kid pulled up a list of names, many with addresses next to them, and an amount of crypto-currency. A link next to that led to a plain QR code.

"Once a kill is confirmed and the payment is made, the entry is deleted," said Tanner. "The name, the QR code, all of it disappears without a trace."

Logan rubbed his hand around his neck.

"And how do you join the Four-Twenty Xanax Mafia?"

"It's not really something you join," he said. "It's more like a brand. There's message boards where a bunch of them hang out while they get high and play video games. They'll post memes and that kind of thing. There's some main guys and if they get to know you and if you're cool, they'll game with you online."

Tanner navigated to the message board he was talking about. All the posts were absurd humour and tough guy posturing.

An anime meme, videos of skateboard wipeouts, swearing back and forth.

There was also an audio feed as they chatted with each other.

"I got some new kicks today," said one kid, his voice crackling over a low bandwidth call.

"What kind?" asked another, his voice also crackling in the same way. Static filled the space in the time where there was no speaking.

"That satisfy your fuckin' foot fetish?" said another voice.

A bunch of them laughed.

"Yo, shut the fuck up, these shoes are the real thing," said the kid. "These are like two hundred and fifty dollar shoes."

"You got more shoes than a girl, man," said one of the kids.

They laughed and talked smack to each other.

"You doing anything today?"

"Man, I'm too high. Just going to lay around. Play some Battlefield. If I can even move the controller. I feel like a fucking puddle."

Each word took a while to enunciate and force out of his lungs.

He posted a picture of a mound of Xanax pills in a blue bowl to the message board.

"Do you know these kids?"

"No," said Tanner, like he had already explained it. "No one's stupid enough to use their real names. You come up with a username and that's it. And some people hang out online and play video games and whatever."

"Why'd you attack me with a fucking sword?" asked Logan.

"Because I don't have a gun yet," said Tanner, as though it were obvious. "And I thought it would be cool for my first kill."

Cliff huffed and puffed and wandered to the far corner of the room. He waved Logan over.

"I think we should keep him here for a few more days," whispered Cliff.

"What? Are you nuts? We have to call the police," Logan whispered back.

"There's more he's not telling us."

"And then what? What then, Cliff, after we've held a kid hostage and tortured him for days? What then?"

Cliff looked Logan in the eyes and twitched an eyebrow.

"What the —" started Logan.

"Can I go home now?" asked the kid.

"Holy fuck," said Cliff. He strode over and pulled Tanner off the couch by the collar and threw him onto the floor. He kicked the kid in the ribs three times until Logan got in front of him and pushed him away.

"What are you doing?" asked Cliff.

"What am I doing? What the fuck are you doing?" said Logan.

"This kid tried to kill you."

"Just fuck off Cliff. It's fine, OK? I got this."

"You don't got this."

"I got this."

"You're nuts," said Cliff.

"You're fucking batshit insane."

Cliff got hostile and looked confused about who he should punch.

Logan opened the door.

"Just go, OK? Go home."

Logan shoved Cliff out the door. He listened to the sound of Cliff complaining and muttering recede down the hall.

He looked back at Tanner on the floor. He was either unconscious or playing dead.

22

The police interview room was still cold enough to store raw chicken. It gave Logan goosebumps and he folded his arms on the bare table in front of him. Overhead, one of the fluorescent lights flickered.

The door opened and Detective Darius Days and his partner Detective Bob Harrison stepped into the room. Detective Harrison wore a green golf shirt this time with his badge hanging around his neck. He took his quiet post in the corner and folded his arms.

Detective Days dragged a chair over with his foot and sat down across from Logan.

"Looks like you and Cliff made acquaintances," he said. "What did I tell you about talking to him?"

"I don't know," said Logan.

"My colleagues are talking to Cliff on the other side of this wall," he said. "And in the room after that is the kid you guys pumped the pumpernickel out of. One of you is going to start telling the truth about what's going on here. A bit of advice—usually when that happens, the other two are in big trouble. So I highly recommend being the first one to talk."

"I'm not hiding anything."

Detective Harrison kept his arms folded and looked Logan up and down.

"That's good," said Days. "Why don't you tell me what happened from the beginning?"

"I was at home. There was a knock at the door. When I opened it that kid swung a sword at my head. He came at me and I managed to subdue him. When I had subdued him, I called Cliff over."

"Uh huh. Why the duct tape?"

"So he wouldn't keep trying to kill me."

"Uh huh. Why'd you call Cliff over?"

"I thought the kid might know something about what happened to Cliff's wife. I figured he should know."

"How come you and Cliff are such good buddies all of a sudden?"

"I ended up asking him if he saw a Corvette around. I guess he needed someone to talk to."

"Uh huh. That kid you guys beat up is only seventeen. A minor. Suppose I arrested you for assault and battery of a minor. What would you think of that?"

"That kid attacked me in my own home, so I would think that's pretty fucked up."

"What do you think Cliff is telling my colleagues in the other room right now?"

"I don't really give a shit," said Logan. "He's batshit crazy. If he says anything that makes sense, I'd love to hear about it myself."

"And what do you think that seventeen year old kid is saying?"

"Asking for his mom? How the fuck am I supposed to know?"

"That's more or less accurate," said Days. "What do you know about his kid Tanner?"

"I know he's not the sharpest crayon in the box," said Logan. "Tell me, did he have a QR code sticker on him when you searched him?"

Days and Harrison exchanged a look.

"Why do you ask? Why would he be carrying a QR code sticker?"

"He thinks he's part of some gang," said Logan. "The Four-Twenty Xanax Mafia. It's sort of a social media thing. But there's a list on the dark web they use."

"Hold up. Hold up. The Four-Twenty Xanax Mafia. What is that?"

"I don't know," said Logan. "They post pictures of themselves in Vegas with nice cars. Girls in bikinis. Pose with stacks of money and drugs. That kind of thing. They hashtag it with Four-Twenty Xanax Mafia."

Days tilted his head to one side and semi-closed one eye as he processed the information.

"Anyway, there's a list," said Logan. "On the dark web. It's a list of people that pays out in crypto-currency if you assassinate them."

"I'm sorry, what?" said Days. "Where is this list?"

"On the dark web."

"Where on the dark web?"

"I don't know. That's what Tanner told us. They find a name on the list. They go and kill that person and put the QR code next to the kill. They take a picture of it and submit it. Once it's verified, crypto-currency is sent to their account anonymously."

"Are you on this list?"

"It certainly appears so," said Logan.

"Who runs this list? The Four-Twenty Xanax Mafia?"

"Sort of? Tanner made it sound fairly automatic. Like it pulls names from other lists."

"Other lists," said Days. "What other lists?"

"You don't know about the lists?" asked Logan. "People keep lists and share notes and gossip about everyone they know?"

"Why don't you tell me about it?"

"You must know what I'm talking about," said Logan. "People keep spreadsheets on the internet and compile notes about everybody. It's like a douchebag central intelligence."

"Where can I find these lists?"

"You have to know what I'm talking about," said Logan. "You're a cop."

"We keep our own tabs on people," said Days. "So where can I see one of these lists?"

"I don't know," said Logan. "I don't have access to them."

"So you can't show me one of these lists?"

"No," said Logan. "I can't."

Days stretched his hand around his brow to massage his temples.

"Tell me what happened again from the beginning," said Days.

"Ugh," said Logan, who then told the story again of the kid coming to his door and trying to kill him with a broadsword. They fought. He bound him with tape. He called Clifford over. They made the kid tell them about the dark web list and the Four-Twenty Xanax Mafia. Clifford ran hot and flew out of control.

When Logan finished Detective Days said, "Hang tight. I'll be back in a bit."

Days got up and left the room. Logan crossed his arms on the table and rested his head on them.

A long while went by. Logan may have dozed off. Maybe not.

When Detective Days entered the room again, Logan sat upright. Days pulled up the chair and leaned forward on the table.

"Here's the deal," he said. "We're letting the kid go."

"He tried to kill me," said Logan.

"Yeah, but it looks like he got the worst of it. He's being cooperative. He's got good parents who said they'd keep him under lock and key. And we can't try him as an adult anyway. If we take this to court, we have to bring you in too. You would have to tell a judge you kicked the ever-loving strawberry milkshake out of a teenager and you don't seem the worse for wear. How's that going to look?"

"I was defending myself. Cliff is the one who beat the hell out of him."

Logan almost yelled it and the muscles in his arms seized up and he slapped the table with both hands before resting his forehead on it to try to breathe out the frustration.

"I know, I know. Calm down. We're going to keep a close eye on him. But look, I'm going to give you one more chance to tell me everything you know about this Four-Twenty Xanax Mafia."

"Or else what?"

"Or else next time I'm not letting you walk out of here. My patience is running very thin right now, Logan."

"I've told you everything I know."

Detective Harrison squinted and bobbed his head to the left and then to the right while he thought about something. Detective Days looked at him. Harrison screwed up his mouth, scrunched his nose, and wiggled his moustache in such a way it communicated something to Days. Days nodded.

"Alright, let's go," said Days.

Days escorted Logan out the door and into the hall.

"Just so you know, we're going to hang on to Cliff a little longer," said Days.

"OK," said Logan.

"You can catch up with him some other time."

"Whatever."

They made their way through the network of hallways to the main lobby of the police station. The homeless man was back at the front desk, still accusing the officer of hiding the existence of space aliens from the public. The tired looking officer suggested he fill out a complaint form.

"No one would take it seriously," said the man.

"You're probably right about that," said the officer.

Right before they reached the door, Days stopped and clutched Logan's elbow.

"You're in danger," said Days. He looked Logan right in the eye. "Stop it with all this. Let it go. Your brother-in-law has other cars. Just drop the Corvette. Leave it to us."

"I'll think about it," said Logan.

He leaned against the heavy glass door.

"Hey Logan," said Days. Logan paused and Days pointed a finger straight between Logan's eyes. "If you find that Stingray, you call me. For sure. Alright?"

Logan nodded and pushed his way out onto the street.

Logan took the 60 bus out of downtown. A teenager sat at the back of the bus with his backpack on his lap and watched Logan make his way down the centre aisle. Logan took a side-facing seat by the back door to keep an eye on the kid.

A couple seats away from the kid a man in a dark suit also seemed to be watching Logan. Logan kept an eye on him too. He kept an eye on both of them through the whole trip but they did nothing and Logan exited the bus at Pulse Casino, along Argyll Road surrounded by industrial lots and cheap hotels.

It was the middle of the afternoon and cars trickled into the parking lot. The woman at the window seemed to give Logan a funny look as he dug out the last of his money and exchanged it for poker chips.

"Good luck," she said.

He ignored whatever her look was about and slunk his way over to the poker room.

The poker tables filled up. Logan scrounged a seat at the back end of the room with a mixed bag of pallid and unshaven faces.

The dealer slid the cards across the table in a relaxed manner. Smooth and unhurried. Logan settled into the rhythm and sunk down into his seat.

The big blind orbited the table and dragged the small blind around in its wake.

Logan folded on junk hands, stayed in the neighbourhood of suited faces, and generally managed to hang in there for a good while but eventually his chips dwindled away. The other players around the table looked at him solemnly, a sorry look in their faces. They too could recognize it wasn't Logan's day.

Eventually most of Logan's chips evaporated and before it was too late he scooped up his last couple chips and walked back to the the cashier's window.

The woman at the window wore a black cotton shirt with buttons on the collar and 'Pulse Casino' embroidered on it. She had big curly 80s bangs hanging over her forehead. She caught eye contact with him, as though she were looking for something inside his eyes, and then broke it while she opened her till. It rang as it opened. She unwrapped a paper band off a wad of bills and slid them in the till.

"The weather's nice," she said as she pulled out a couple bills for Logan.

"I guess it's alright," he said.

"Good time to get out of town," she said, still holding his bills in her hand.

"I guess so."

"Is there anywhere you like to go on vacation?"

"I don't really get out of town too much."

She counted out the couple bills onto the counter and held eye contact with him again.

"You should," she said. "You should get out of town for a while."

"That would be nice," said Logan, swiping up the money and folding it into his wallet. He lingered to stare back at her, to see if she was trying to say something.

"Take care," she said.

Logan pushed his way out of the front revolving door of the casino, across the parking lot, and crossed the street to a strip mall bar called Neighbours. He sat at the bar. A few old-timers squabbled about a football game at a table halfway down the bar and leered at Logan like they owned the place. Otherwise the bar was empty. The music was turned down to a barely perceptible level.

The smell of urinal pucks emanated from the washrooms where the door was propped open with a bucket and mop.

A woman behind the bar in a plaid shirt with the sleeves rolled up to the elbows leaned toward him and addressed Logan with a casual uptick of her head.

"Gold Star," said Logan.

She walked to the fridge behind her, popped the cap off a bottle of beer and brought it back to him.

"You want a menu?" she asked.

"No, thanks."

"That's good," she said. "The cook didn't come in and I don't feel like turning on the grill."

She disappeared into the back and Logan sipped on his beer. Clanking and banging noises came out of the kitchen. After a while, she came back with a bit of sweat on her face. She wiped her face on her sleeve and sat on a stool next to Logan.

"You at the casino today?" she asked.

"For a little bit."

"Win big?"

"Not this time," said Logan.

"There's always next time," she said. "My mom won a couple grand on the machines a couple weeks ago."

"Good for her," said Logan.

"She was pretty excited," she said. "Any plans for summer?"

"Working, mostly," said Logan.

"You should get out of town," she said.

"Should I?"

"Can't work all the time," she said. "Take a break. Get out of town for a bit."

"Someone was just telling me the same thing," he said.

"Must be a sign," she said.

Logan leaned back to get a better look at her.

She knocked on the bar twice as a sort of goodbye, stood up off her stool and made herself busy in the back again.

Logan finished his beer and put the empty bottle on a ten dollar bill on the bar and walked outside.

The brightness outside halted him in his tracks. There were no clouds in the sky and the streets radiated back the heat from the sun. He walked up the sidewalk along a construction yard back toward the bus stop. A white full-length cargo van pulled alongside Logan.

The driver got out. A large man with round shoulders in a mucky blue hi-vis jacket lumbered up to Logan. Several days worth of stubble covered his jaw and his eyes were cloudy and dim. Before Logan could react, the man slugged Logan in stomach. Logan bent over and grabbed onto the man's sleeves while he collected his breath.

"What's going on?" asked Logan, hanging on to the sleeves of the man's jacket. "What do you want?"

"Get in," said the guy.

The man grabbed Logan's shirt with one hand and pulled Logan staggering to the back of the van. He opened the back door of the van with his free hand.

A few loose tools, a power generator, and cargo straps lined the edges of the van. A black metal partition separated the back cargo space from the driver and passenger seat in the front.

Logan climbed in and the guy shut the door behind him.

23

Logan sat with his back against the metal partition. The cargo van picked up speed and pulled onto the freeway. Logan bent his knees slightly and put his feet flat on the floor and balanced himself with his hands at his sides. The van braked with a lurch here and there, the driver braking half a second too late each time.

The smooth vibrations of the highway eventually gave way to the rumble of dirt under the tires. The van curved around in a long arc, the rumble of gravel crunching under the tires, and then stopped. Logan heard both the driver and passenger doors open and close. The driver walked around and opened the back door. Sunlight poured in and only his silhouette showed in the doorway.

The driver put his hand around the back of Logan's neck as he climbed out. As his eyes adjusted he came to see they were in an empty dirt parking lot next to a rail yard. Concrete barriers ran along the perimeter of the lot and on the other side of them, rusty train cars with graffiti splashed along the sides lined up along several rows of tracks.

Logan spun around. The driver gripped Logan's jacket near his shoulder. Behind him stood the man with a million-dollar smile on the For Sale sign in Cliff's front yard - Darcy Hannigan. But he wasn't smiling.

"Hi, Logan," said Hannigan. "I'm here to make you a deal."

Logan clenched his fists.

"A once in a lifetime deal," said Hannigan. "It's easier than sin and it will change your life."

Logan tugged his shoulder back to get the big boy to let go but he didn't.

"Settle down," said Hannigan. "I'm trying to help you. Here's the deal. Stop looking for the Corvette. Just drop it. All you have to do is nothing."

"And?" said Logan.

"And in return," said Hannigan. "You know the lists. I'll erase you from all the lists. Forever."

"You can edit all the lists?"

"All the ones that matter," he said. "Think of that. A fresh start. That's a pretty good deal. No one has been edited off the lists before. And all you have to do is nothing."

A hot growl curdled up from the back of Logan's throat.

"I want editing privileges," he said.

"I can't do that. You're a liability. You could delete everything. But I can delete you off them. Forever. You're lucky, you know. No one else gets this deal. You can live your life with a blank slate. Apply for jobs. When you meet people they won't be able to look up your deep, dark secrets. You can tell them whatever you want. You can tell them you're the Sultan of Brunei. I don't give a shit. It's gone. Over. I can put a filter on the lists where your name won't even show up if someone tries to type it in. Just leave the Corvette alone. How's that sound?"

Logan gave something like a nod and grimaced as he processed what was going on.

Hannigan nodded at his big friend.

The driver clocked Logan across the face a couple times. A couple heavy blows with something in his hand that Logan wasn't ready for. A wrench? Something. The world spun. The guy punched him in the gut, and threw Logan to the ground. He kicked Logan once more in the stomach.

"Think about it," said Hannigan. "But if you fuck with me, we'll beat you until you're close enough to see where your life ends and the darkness begins. How about that?"

Hannigan and the other guy got back in the van. Logan lay on his side and watched the van drive away. The he rolled onto his back in the dirt and rested there a while.

He tried to sit up but the world spun and he collapsed back down onto his side. He lay flat and took a breath. He rolled himself up onto his hands and knees and tried to stand up again, and again the world spun and his legs buckled and he pitched forward onto his hands and knees. He rolled onto his back and closed his eyes.

Logan lay in the gravel under the hot sun. Blood hardened against his top lip. A layer of dirt settled on his sun-burnt face.

His phone rang. It vibrated in his pocket. He dug it out. It was Clare.

He stayed on his back and pulled the phone up to his ear.

"Good news," she sang. "I got accepted to school."

"That's awesome," said Logan. "Congratulations."

"You don't sound like you're jumping up and down," she said. Teasing, mostly.

"I'm excited for you," said Logan. "That's really great."

"What's going on?"

"Nothing," he said. "Hey, are you free at all? I'm stuck on the West side. I don't suppose you can pick me up."

There was a moment while she considered the tone of his voice.

"Where are you?"

"I'm in a parking lot by a train yard. Just off the Yellowhead and, I think, 156th. There's a big industrial park on the other side of the tracks."

"What are you doing there?"

"Long story," said Logan.

"Are you OK?"

"Yeah, I'm good. Just kind of got stuck out here."

Dust from the gravel entered Logan's mouth and he coughed. It made the bruised ribs and abdominal muscles clench and he wheezed.

"Are you sure you're OK? You don't sound OK."

"Some guys kind of roughed me up a bit. It's fine though."

"Logan."

"No, it's not like that. This was just random."

"Were you gambling?"

"Not really. I passed through the casino briefly but this has nothing to do with that."

"Logan."

"Can I just get a ride please?"

"No," she said. She started to sob. "I'm sorry, Logan. I can't keep doing this. I'm sorry. Good bye."

She hung up.

Logan let his arm fall by his side and he lay on his back looking at clouds drift into view.

He lifted his phone again and phoned Cliff.

"What are you doing right now?"

"Charging my phone in the alley behind a Quik Lube," said Cliff. "And trying to find Waldo in this book. I don't even think he's on this fucking page. Medieval times? This is bullshit."

"I kind of ran into some trouble. Again. I don't suppose you could give me a lift?"

24

Cliff's pickup truck emerged at the top of the service road and came rumbling down the gravel ramp to the empty lot. He found Logan sitting on the ground and resting his back against a concrete barrier that separated the lot from the train tracks.

He pulled up and got out and sallied over to Logan.

"You look like shit, man," said Cliff. He reached down and hoisted Logan to his feet. "What you do? Go on another of those hot dates of yours?"

"Your real estate agent kicked the hell out of me. Or at least, his buddy did."

They climbed in his truck and Cliff started it up. The radio jingle for 100.3 FM "The Bear" blasted out the speakers with a grizzly bear growl followed by a hard rock song. Cliff skidded back up the ramp and back onto the freeway.

"What do you mean?" asked Cliff.

"The real estate agent on the sign in your yard. They threw me in a van, brought me here, kicked the hell out of me."

"What for?"

"The Corvette. They want me to leave it alone. I don't know why it matters to them so much."

"It's not about the car," said Cliff. "It's the lists. You stepped over the line and you aren't supposed to know about the lists. They want you to forget about them. Well fuck 'em. We're going to get that Corvette and drive it right up their ass."

Logan looked away.

"Oh come on. Don't tell me you're backing down, man. You can't. It just means you're getting closer. Once you have the car, this is all over."

"No it's not," said Logan. "The lists are always going to be there."

"So what?"

"I don't need to be hospitalized for a '76 Stingray."

"They killed Brooke," said Cliff. "I need your help."

"What am I supposed to do?" said Logan. "I don't know where the car is."

"You're close," said Cliff. "You have to do this."

"I can't do it," said Logan.

"You're just feeling beat up."

"I am beat up."

"Let's get out of here."

Cliff stopped at a liquor store on 97th street called 97 Liquor. Logan stayed in the truck while Cliff disappeared behind the caged doors and a little while later came out with a case of Gold Star and a bottle in a brown paper bag. He tucked them in the back of the truck up by the cab. Then he climbed in and they drove through Chinatown and into downtown, lurching their way forward in traffic between blocks of skyscrapers.

It was the end of the business day and Cliff pulled into a multi-level parking lot, the only vehicle going up against the stream of other cars spiraling downward and going home for the day.

"Where are you taking me?"

"Somewhere to drink."

Round and round he drove until they pulled up to the very top floor of the parking lot where the view opened up to show the city skyline all around them.

Cliff pulled a bottle of cheap whiskey out of the paper bag, cracked the top, and flicked the cap over the edge of the parking lot into the city beyond.

He pulled a swig from the bottle and passed it to Logan.

"I'm good," said Logan.

"Drinky, drinky," said Cliff gesturing with his hands to tip the bottle up.

Logan took a sip from the bottle. One sip turned into a couple more sips. Cliff reached in through the truck window to turn the ignition half way to get the radio going, more hard rock from 100.3 'The Bear'.

He emerged from his truck again with some papers and a bag of pot and loped to the edge of the parking lot and looked down at the street below. The after-work crowd scurried their way down the street, some of them filtering into a little Tudor-style pub across the street from the parkade. Cliff rolled a joint on the ledge, shoved the papers and pot in his pocket, and stuck the joint in his mouth and lit it.

"I'm going to move out to the bush," he said and then exhaled smoke out toward the skyscrapers. "Once I figure out who did this to Brooke. I want to know who did it and why. I need to know for sure. And then I'm gone."

"It would feel good to get out of town."

"I'm gone forever. It's a different world. I don't want no part of it."

"How would you live?"

"Hunt. Do cash jobs for folks and buy groceries that way. There's a guy who said he'd sell me his truck camper for cheap. I need to get off the grid. Random murderers coming to find you with all this technology and getting paid in crypto? No thanks. I'm out.

"There's a little gully I know about, out near Germansen Landing in the mountains. You drive up an old forest service road, and it pulls into a valley where there's a waterfall and a lake and you can see all the mountains. Ain't nobody around to bother you. It's paradise. We used to play around there when we were kids. We'd bury treasure for each other. Metal tins and coins and toys and that sort of thing. It was perfect. God's country.

"Yup. I'll take my chances with the bears and the wolves and the weather. But I'll be free, man. Help people out in the nearby towns. Breathe in the mountain air and wake up each morning and decide what I'd like to do. Not have to report to anyone. That's real living.

Maybe I'll go see if I can find any of our old buried treasure. It'd be something to do anyway."

Logan leaned over the back of Cliff's truck and opened the case of Gold Star sitting inside. Cracked open a can and took a sip. Pulled his phone out of his pocket and scrolled through the pictures of CoDPimp and the 420 Xanax Mafia.

"Me and Brooke talked about moving but never did anything about it," Cliff continued. "I think she wanted to move. She didn't ever feel completely safe. But she also felt tied down to that house somehow."

Cliff walked back from the wall, and leaned on the other side of the truck opposite Logan.

"Where do you think that car is?" Cliff asked. His eyes dug at Logan while he talked.

Logan looked away.

"It could be anywhere," said Logan. "I can't find it."

Cliff got angry.

"You can," said Cliff. "Why not?"

"I just can't, OK?" said Logan. "I can't."

"You're not thinking right," said Cliff. "You can find it. You're thinking too much about yourself and these other people who don't matter. Think about the car."

"It's not that easy," said Logan.

"Nothing's easy," said Cliff, raising his voice. "Just do it. I know you, man. I can see you know how to figure this out and you're just not doing it is all."

"Why are you putting this on me? Why don't you find the car?"

"Because my brain doesn't work like that. I'm meant for something else. Being alone in the woods like an animal, maybe. But you, you're different. Your brain has radar for this sort of thing."

"It's not like that."

"Why isn't it? It's like you see things different but then refuse to help yourself."

"Fuck off. You don't know me. I'm sick of people projecting their shit on me. Why can't people let me live my life?"

"Live your life, man. No one's stopping you."

"Look, my whole life I've been on the other side looking in. I'm not one of these people that go about their lives like every day is just another day. All 'la dee da'. Every minute of every day feels extremely fucked up to me and nothing is going to change that. People going to work. People going on vacation. Relaxing in front of a movie. None of it makes any sense to me and whenever I have to spend time with people, I have to pretend like it does. And all I've ever wanted was for it to feel normal for me too because everybody else seems to get by OK and I feel like if I could make life feel normal for me then I could get by OK too but I can't. I can't do it."

Logan's voice warbled and he slunk away, red-faced. He wiped his face with his hand and turned his back to Cliff.

Cliff nodded.

"OK but why don't you just find the Corvette though?"

"Fuck off," said Logan and walked away toward the other side of the parking lot. Cliff laughed.

"I'm just joking. Busting your balls, man."

"I think my sister would be better off if I was out of her life," said Logan. He slid down the concrete barrier and sat on the ground. Cliff tore a couple more cans of beer out of the box in the back of the truck and followed Logan to the edge of the parking lot. He sat down next to Logan against the concrete barrier and passed him a beer.

"Yeah," said Cliff.

"This is where you say, 'Don't be stupid. Your sister needs you.'"

Cliff snorted a kind of laugh.

"I don't know," he said. "Maybe she would be better off. You're kind of weird, to be honest. But I'm sure she wants you around."

Logan shook his head and smiled a little and looked up at the office towers around them.

"Whenever I'm sitting around talking with people," Logan continued. "I'm always waiting for them to break and start laughing. Or give a wink. Like everyone's just pretending to take the conversation seriously. But they never do. They talk about stupid movies and buying shitty plastic cars or parrot whatever political points they get from whatever shitty news website. Or they're talking about how important their job is. And I'm always waiting for that moment where everybody laughs and drops it but they never do."

"I think I know what you mean," said Cliff. He sipped from the can and thought about it.

They both looked up at the office towers around them and watched a floor of office lights turn off. Then another. And then a row of office lights would turn on as janitorial staff did their rounds.

"Hey," said Cliff. "If you could have any kind of car, what would it be?"

"Datsun 510 with a V8 dropped into it," said Logan. Cliff's bottom lip stiffened.

"Good answer," he said. "You one of those guys that's into drifting?"

"It's like a little armoured shell. You can cruise around town in it but also take it out and bag the shit out of it."

They both nodded at the thought.

"What about you?"

Cliff thought about it.

"You know the Subaru BRAT?"

"I don't think so," said Logan.

"It's a four-wheel drive car but it's got a back like a truck."

"Like an El Camino?"

"Kind of, but all-terrain. You can even put a camper on it. Roll bars. Bull bars on the front."

An old metal song came on the radio and Cliff jumped up off the ground. He opened the driver's side door and reached inside to turn the radio up. He chugged the rest of his beer, crunched the can in his hand and threw it over the edge of the parkade wall. He air-guitared along to the radio. Logan scrolled through his phone, flicking through pictures of the 420 Xanax Mafia.

He stopped at the picture of the kid on his front lawn with the Rottweiler. A grainy tangerine sky behind him. Orange sticks in the ground in the lot behind him casting long shadows across the street.

"Listen to this part," said Cliff.

"Holy shit," said Logan.

"I know, right?"

"No."

Cliff wasn't paying attention. He was wrapped up in the guitar riffs of the song.

"I think I know where the car is," said Logan. He stood up and kept scrolling through his phone.

"Here," said Cliff. "This part."

The music lifted and hesitated before dropping into a heavy drum breakdown.

"Cliff," shouted Logan. "Look at this. I think I know where the car is."

Cliff snapped out of his trance and stared at Logan. Logan walked over toward Cliff while staring down at his phone and then looking up at the buildings around them, looking for a gap between them to see the horizon.

25

Cliff rolled the truck back down around the parkade levels and when they reached the ground floor, he stopped at the exit before turning onto the street.

"West side of town?" he asked. "Why?"

"Look at these shadows," said Logan. He held up his phone and Cliff leaned over to look at the photo posted by CoDPimp.

"What about them?"

"Look how long they are," said Logan. Behind the kid standing in on his front lawn with a Rottweiler was a muddy lot with orange sticks pointing out of the ground to indicate power lines. The low setting sun cast long shadows from the power markers stretching all the way across the road.

"So?"

"So there's not many places where you're going to get shadows like that."

"Why not?"

"Because bigger stuff gets in the way. It just turns into one big shadow by the time the sun gets that low. But not where this kid is. Long shadows. Sun sets in the west. This kid is in a newer residential development on the west side of town."

"Which one?" asked Cliff.

"Let's start driving west," said Logan. "We'll figure it out."

Cliff pulled out of the parkade, steered them out of the downtown core and onto Stony Plain Road. Logan tapped his thumb against the tips of each of his fingers.

Stony Plain Road swooped away from downtown, over the river, and joined onto the Anthony Henday ring road circling the city.

"Where next, Columbus?"

"I'm thinking," said Logan. He studied the photo on his phone.

"Hang on," said Cliff. He swung sharply to an off-ramp up onto where the Whitemud crosses over the Henday and pulled over to the edge of the road. Passing cars honked at them. They both got out of the truck and surveyed the west end of town.

A tangerine glow stretched across the horizon to the west with the first dark shades of purple approaching from the east. Ribbons of gold rippled in long streamers under waves of watery blue. Logan studied the photo of CoDPimp. Cliff looked over his shoulder. They both looked up at the position of the setting sun.

"What do you think?" said Cliff. "Somewhere over there?"

He pointed to his right in the direction of the sun.

"There's some newer communities that way past the golf course," said Logan.

They both grunted in agreement and got back in the truck and Cliff steered back down the Whitemud to the edge of town.

They crept along 215th street. Traffic was quiet. Eventually the road ran out of streetlights. Undeveloped grassland stretched out on the right side of the road with warehouse lights blinking in the distance. Turnoffs on the left side of the road curled behind shale walls holding up each community's name. Cedar Glen. Hamlet. Castle View.

Cliff pulled up to the entrance of each community and they took a look at each one, comparing it to the picture on the phone. Eventually 215th stretched off into farmland and he stopped the truck in the middle of the road and pulled a four-point U-turn back around to take a second pass at each neighbourhood.

Each community held similar looking homes or the wooden frames of homes in development. Each house stood atop a one or two-car garage. Large living room windows stretched up a full storey on the front facades.

Cliff pulled into Chilton Estates and paused by the entrance gate. They scanned each house and the curve of the sidewalks and rolled quietly along the road looping through the centre of the community.

"Nope," said Logan.

They drove on to the next neighbourhood. Chestnut Grove. The streets held houses much the same as the first although the sod hadn't been laid yet. Some of the lots held only the wooden frame of houses in development. Logan tipped his head from side to side as he thought about it. Cliff pulled in and rolled around the main loop.

"Fifty-fifty," said Logan.

It went like this for several other communities. Aizlewood. Spruce Valley. Whitcombe Towne.

They rolled along quietly and when there was a curve in the sidewalk similar to the photo, Logan held the phone up and they both examined the photo and compared it to the road in front of them.

When Cliff pulled into the next community of Hewer Downs, something felt different. Logan tapped his thumb against his fingertips but neither of them said anything. Cliff rolled along. Logan pointed to a quiet cul de sac of completed homes stationed around the curved sidewalk. All of them quiet with darkened windows.

Logan didn't say anything. Cliff took his foot off the brake and was about to heave the steering wheel around when Logan said, "Wait."

Cliff stopped.

"I like this one."

Cliff rolled them in.

"There," said Logan. "Right in the middle."

At the bowl end of the cul-de-sac was a dark house with a two-car garage. The lights were off.

Cliff parked a few houses away and turned off the ignition.

"They've built more houses since this photo was taken," said Logan. He swiveled his body to hold his phone up to the neighbour's house.

"That one there had these sticks coming out of the ground to create these long shadows," said Logan.

Cliff looked over his shoulder.

"The shadows are at a different angle," said Cliff.

"This photo was taken at a different time of year," said Logan. "The sun was in a different position. Over there."

Logan pointed to the left of the house.

Cliff looked back at the dark house in the middle.

"So this is the one?"

Logan nodded.

"Are you sure?" asked Cliff.

"It's the odds-on favourite," said Logan.

They both got out of the truck. Cliff leaned into the back of his truck and pulled out an orange-handled ball peen hammer.

"Come on," he whispered.

"What are you doing?" Logan whispered.

"Let's go," said Cliff. He trotted up to the neighbour's hedge next to the house and crouched next to it. Logan followed behind and knelt down next to him.

"What are you —" Logan repeated but Cliff held up a hand. Cliff gestured with military hand signals. A circle in the air, a slight wave, two fingers pointed toward his eyes, then a chopping motion toward the door. Cliff hustled over to the side of the house in a crouched military position and waved for Logan to follow.

Logan did as he did. Cliff slid along the wall and stalked his way up to the front door and kept to one side, placing his shoulder to one side. Logan followed and leaned into the opposite side of the front door.

Cliff held his breath as he listened. It was silent.

He tried the door handle. It was unlocked.

He pushed open the door and they both leaned in to look inside.

Then teeth and snarl and fury. A barking Rottweiler leapt off the stair entry and bounded toward them with its teeth bared. It leapt into Logan's chest, knocking him backward off the front step.

Logan landed on his back and the dog stood on his collarbone. Saliva sprayed from the dog's mouth as it barked and gnashed its teeth. Logan tried to roll it off but he hadn't had time to absorb the impact of the fall and the dog was all muscle and coursing veins.

Then thud.

Cliff swung the hammer in a golf swing arc into the side of the dog's head. It was stunned and Cliff kicked the dog off. Logan jumped up and braced for another attack from the dog.

The dog turned and reared, preparing to pounce, but it swayed. One leg buckled and it staggered on its feet like a drunk. It dipped to the other side. The dog whimpered and ran off under the neighbour's bushes.

"Come on," said Cliff.

"Let's get the fuck out of here," said Logan.

"It's gone now," said Cliff. He stared intently at Logan and gave him a sharp wave to follow. Then he stepped inside the house. Logan followed.

An empty sitting room met them to the right, completely unfurnished. Plush cream-coloured carpet looked as though no one had ever set foot on it.

They tip-toed up the steps to the kitchen. Condiments and cardboard packages for microwavable food covered the counters along with empty bottles of vodka and cans of energy drinks. Dirty dishes piled up in the sink.

From the kitchen, they could see a hall led to a few steps down into a den where the door was open and, inside, a video game was put on pause on a large screen TV.

BRRAAATTT.

Bullets everywhere. A muzzle flash sprayed out from the corner like a strobe light flame. A clinking of shells. The cupboards opened up behind them exploding in splinters of wood.

A kid sprung out from behind the corner holding a mini Uzi machine gun. He wore basketball shorts and a track suit jacket and a golf visor. CoDPimp. The kid sprayed bullets at them. They ducked behind the kitchen island. Bullets tore at the other side of the kitchen island. Cans of energy drink exploded. The fridge ruptured with a series of bullet holes.

Cliff opened a drawer and pulled out a steak knife. He pinched the blade between his fingers and flung it in the direction of the kid. Missed.

"Come and get me, you fucking shit," said Cliff. He stood up and ran out of the kitchen and back down the stairs toward the basement. The kid chased after him.

Logan was flat on his stomach and peeked around the kitchen island as he saw Cliff jump down the stairs. The kid followed down the stairs, gun drawn.

Logan swore and thumped the ground with his fists before lifting himself and running toward them.

CoDPimp hesitated on the steps. He turned in time to see Logan at the top of the stairs. Logan jumped and tackled him. He wrapped his arm around the kid's neck and hauled him to the ground.

The kid flung the gun around. Logan wrestled the gun hand to the ground and knelt on his arm long enough for Cliff to fly in and drive his knee into the kid's face.

The kid dropped the gun. Cliff knelt on top of the kid and pummeled the kid's face with his fist a few times.

He stood up and put his hands under the kid's armpits and dragged him backwards into the next room, another kind of gaming den with a pool table and a dart board. A large TV sat at the end next to a small bar with sports jerseys framed and mounted on the wall.

He hoisted the kid onto a wooden chair. He stomped down onto the base of a floor lamp and pulled the electrical cord out of it. He wrapped it around the kid's wrists and bound him tightly to the chair.

"Grab me the cord out of that one," said Cliff pointing at another lamp on a side table next to the couch. Logan put it under his arm and yanked the cord out.

"Tie up his feet," said Cliff.

Logan knelt down and tied the cord around the kid's ankles.

"Cliff, stop," said Logan. "Let's call the police."

Cliff spun around with hatred in his eyes. He pushed Logan in the chest hard enough so that Logan reeled backward into the wall behind him.

"You can shut the fuck up," said Cliff. Cliff raised the hammer to threaten Logan. "Or you can sit next to that kid and join him."

Logan put his hands up. Cliff's eyes protruded from his skull and he stood stock still for a moment except for his chest, which heaved up and down.

Logan looked at the kid.

"I just want the car," he said.

The kid's head lolled toward his pocket.

"In my pocket," said the kid.

Logan walked toward him and reached into the jacket pocket of his track suit and pulled out a set of keys.

"Cliff," said Logan. "I think you should stop. Don't do this. There's nothing to be gained."

Cliff kicked over the coffee table in his way and strode toward Logan with the hammer raised halfway beside him and his eyes red with hate.

"Who the fuck are you?" said Cliff. He put a hand around Logan's throat and pushed him back against the wall. Logan tried to swat his arm away but Cliff butted the handle end of the hammer into Logan's chest as message to stop squirming. "Who the fuck are you to tell me what I should and shouldn't do?"

Rage streamed out of his eyes. Logan tried stepping backward but he was already up against the wall.

"I need to talk to Mr. Bigshot here," said Cliff. "Get out of here. Before I decide to not leave any witnesses."

Logan backed slowly out of the room and up the stairs, then stepped up the next set of stairs to the kitchen. His feet marched by themselves.

At the top of the stairs Logan walked down a short hallway to the garage. As he opened the door he heard a fleshy thwack from the basement and the kid moan.

Logan opened the door. Down below on the garage floor was the amethyst blue '76 Corvette Stingray. He descended the stairs and hit the garage door button. It slowly raised to reveal several police cars screaming across the dark cul de sac street and parking at the end of the driveway. The sun had set. Their flashing red and blue lights lit the trees and houses around them. The cars stopped abruptly at the curb blocking the end of the driveway.

Logan got into the Corvette and started it up. He put it in first gear and the car surged forward, unwieldy like a pitbull on the end of a leash. He lurched into the driveway as Detective Darius Days stepped out from his SUV.

Days had his hands up. The doors of other police cars opened and officers got out with their guns drawn.

"Logan," he called out. "Logan. Listen to me. Absolutely not. Get out of the car now. If you get out of the car, I can help you. If you drive away, I can't help you. There's nothing I can do. Do not drive that car, Logan. Get out of the car."

A couple more cops approached the Corvette behind Days with their guns drawn, taking long cautious steps.

Logan couldn't see how many police cars filled the block. Their headlights and red and blue flashers blinded him.

A gun shot rang out from inside the house. A basement light went out and a window smashed.

The cops all retreated back behind the open doors of their vehicles. Days ducked behind the front end of his SUV.

Logan popped the clutch and the roar of the 350 V8 engine rumbled into Logan's guts. There was no burnout. The V8 engine sat so far back over the crossmember Logan was practically tea-bagging it, and it pushed the drive train further down, putting the driver's ass right up against the back tire. Just grip n' rip. And Logan tore across the neighbour's front lawns as he shot off like a rocket around the barricade of police cars.

When he reached the gateway of the neighbourhood, he watched in the rearview mirror as some of the police cars reversed and swung around to pursue him. Logan turned on the radio dial and found something with plenty of electric guitars and synthesizers and then he took off.

The Corvette didn't like corners. It bucked forward like a riled horse. He took a left and shot off down 215th Street with several police cars in pursuit like a school of fish following a Maco shark.

He shot past the last of the streetlights and kept going out into the country. The police caught up and stayed on the back end of the car, lights flashing and sirens blaring. There were four police cars in a line behind him. The closest one swerved toward the back end of his car.

Logan punched the stick shift into fourth gear. The engine opened up like an air raid siren. The car shook and wobbled and Logan grasped the little steering wheel and hung on.

He reached a township road and hit the brakes, pulled the hand brake, and skidded into a long drift into it. He shifted down, then back up.

You don't tell a C3 Corvette how fast to go. A C3 tells you how fast it's going to go and you spend the drive time negotiating with it. The tiny steering wheel demanded Logan's undivided attention and his elbows and shoulders strained to wrench it in the direction he wanted it to go. It made the act of driving active and involved, and at no point did Logan feel entirely in control. At times the steering response became soft and unresponsive and other times it was touchy and temperamental, so on curves in the road he would have to demand the car's obedience and on long straightaways it seemed the slightest gesture might send him over the edge.

But the C3 Stingray isn't a car as we've come to know cars over time. It's no Volvo or Mazda, with anti-lock brakes and parking assist notifications. It's closer to sitting on a goddamn scud missile and trying to steer it with a lasso tied around the front end more than commuting in any modern coupe you can think of. The only reason it's called a car is because it's got four wheels on it, and even those chubby 225/70s felt like an afterthought on the part of the engineers. And when you're hanging onto the centre yellow line while sitting in a rock n' roll torpedo, there's not a lot of time for thinking. And yet, the mind is elevated to a heightened state for its own survival. It still has a way of pondering things on its own time.

It was around the time Logan reached a speed clearly unsafe for everyone involved that the police cars behind him backed off. They retreated in his rear-view so they were about 200 yards behind, then 300. They turned the sirens off but kept the flashers on. They fell further and further back in his rear-view mirror until the red and blue lights were quiet sparkles in the distance, and then eventually they too disappeared behind the dark horizon.

Darkness descended all around him. The highway was a straight line, and he and the Stingray had come to an uneasy truce on how to manage the road ahead. He hugged the yellow line running down the centre of the road and they surged forward, the movement automatic, its own force of nature out of Logan's control.

He was a shark alone in a dark ocean and the waters were still and he reveled in the force of his own perfect propulsion. So unwieldy and volatile it was perfect.

A shark has to move to stay alive. They have no system to pump water over their gills, so to breathe they need to keep swimming to keep water filtering over their gills. And it needs energy to keep moving so it must keep devouring. Always in debt to its own skin.

Finally, Logan was alone. He brought the speed down to something marginally more comfortable. Stars blinked to life in the night sky. He turned the radio off. There was only the chug of the Corvette engine and it filled Logan's insides. Outside of him was darkness and he hugged the yellow line at the centre of the road. The headlights lit up the distance ahead and the distance ahead stayed a constant straight line with the lit up skyscrapers of the city stretching up in the distant dark.

Out in the quiet of the country there was a sense of coming up for air, and he was diving back down to the depths of the city now.

Streetlights appeared on the sides of the highway. The roads were empty. He turned up a ramp onto the main road into the city and that's when he heard the helicopter. The thumping noise grew louder and louder. Logan turned back off the main road onto a service road by a concrete plant. He pulled to the side of the road and reversed up the sloped retaining wall underneath an overpass. He turned off the engine and waited.

A spotlight shone down and probed the Earth like a great finger from the sky. The beam of light flashed on either side of the bridge and up the road. He listened to the thumping propellers hover overhead and then wander about a mile or so away. Then they returned and the spotlight flicked around some more.

For an hour the helicopter roved the area and eventually the thumping faded away to nothing. Logan waited some time longer to be sure before starting up the Stingray and pulling back out onto the road.

Logan kept to back roads and alleys. As he crept out of an alley a police car slinked by. They rolled around the corner and Logan took the next moment to cut out of the alley and down another onto the next block.

He pulled onto the back lot behind Champion City Pawn. Dixie and Trixie bounded around him barking. He patted them on the heads. Got back in the car and rolled it onto the lot. There was stillness when he turned off the ignition. He was aware of the stillness more than he had ever felt it before. He could feel it on his skin.

26

Detective Bob Harrison wore a powder blue golf shirt this time. He sat in the corner of the chilly interview room with his arms folded over the police badge hanging from his neck and studied Logan's face.

Detective Darius Days spent a long time bowed forward with his elbows on his knees, thinking about what he wanted to say. Or maybe he was trying to get Logan to sweat it for a while to see what he would do.

"I've got all day," said Days.

"Me too," said Logan.

"Why don't you tell me what happened from the beginning? What were you doing at that house?"

"I thought the car would be there," said Logan. "I was hanging out with Cliff when we looked at the social media posts of the 420 Xanax Mafia. It sort of clicked from there."

"Back it up," said Days. "I want to revisit this 420 Xanax Mafia. Tell me again who they are."

"From what I can tell it's a bunch of kids who are addicted to drugs and make bad rap music and play video games all day. And they perform low budget freelance hit jobs on people to fund their lifestyle."

"And when Tanner attacked you, that's when you first became aware of the 420 Xanax Mafia?" asked Days.

"Yeah. Pretty much. Tanner told us about the hit list on the dark web."

"Uh huh," said Days. "So you stumble across these kids on social media. How did you know they had the car?"

"Repo man's hunch," said Logan.

"I'm not kidding around," said Days.

"Neither am I."

"So you get this hunch and drive straight to this kid's house," said Days. "You ever meet this kid before?"

"No. I tried contacting him on social media but the kid told me to fuck off."

"How did you know where he lived?"

"I didn't. We drove around looking at the pictures he posted on social media until we figured it out."

"I'm going to be honest with you, Logan. This isn't working for me and I'm going to start losing my patience soon. So far you've told me you magically stumbled across this network of kids, and then you surmised one of these kids had the car, and then you guessed where he lived?"

"More or less," said Logan.

"That doesn't work for me," said Days. He grew visibly angrier. "Your buddy Cliff is dead and I have an eighteen year old kid in serious condition, and you're going to tell me something I can use."

"Cliff's dead?"

"You didn't know that?"

The blood left Logan's face. He curled forward and rested both elbows on the table and scratched the back of his head with his hands.

"No," said Logan. Logan shut his eyes tight as he thought.

The detectives exchanged a glance.

"Cliff's dead," Days repeated. "You don't know how it happened?"

Logan shook his head.

"Well, I can't get into that right now. I want to hear what you know. What happened when you got to the house?"

"We drove there in Cliff's truck. Decided that was the house. We opened the door and a dog attacked me. It jumped on top of me. Cliff hit it with a hammer and it ran away."

"Inside the house?"

"On the front lawn after we opened the front door. Then we went inside. The kid shot at us."

"So you walk in the house. Where were you when you were shot at?"

"In the kitchen. Then Cliff ran into the basement and the kid followed him. I went to the garage and got the car."

"Uh huh. Where'd you get the keys?"

"They were on the dash."

"Uh huh. And you didn't think to check on your buddy Cliff?"

"The kid was shooting at us with a machine gun. I didn't want anything to do with that. I just went to the car. How'd he die?"

"While he was beating the one kid, another kid came out of the spare room with a shotgun and shot him."

Logan let out a long breath.

"We got the other kid that shot him," Days continued. "Seventeen years old. He was co-owner of the house if you can believe that. It's still up in the air on how we're going to charge him. And I am dying to charge you with something except I don't know what would actually stick."

"Are you going to do anything about the lists?"

"We have our guys looking at the hit lists on the dark web," said Days. "From the sounds of things, this hit list you were on was set up on a server in Guyana. It's good news in a way because they are an allied country and we can have this list taken down. You have to understand, the dark web is a pretty nebulous place. If someone sets up another list on a server in, say, the Philippines, there's not a lot we can do about it to be perfectly honest."

"What about the other lists they pull from? The spreadsheets people around here subscribe to?"

"I'll be honest with you. The office of the privacy commissioner will look into them for breaches of protection of privacy law, but there's not a lot we can do about those either. It's not illegal to make a list."

"What about that real estate agent Hannigan? He's deep in the lists. And Talia Bodkins. She subscribes."

"We'll look into it."

"You'll look into it."

"Like I say, it's not illegal to make a list."

"Does Cliff have any family?" asked Logan.

"We're looking," said Days. "Do you want to hear about Brooke?"

"Sure."

"We're in touch with her mom and her sister. We have a guy bringing them up to speed right now. It's a lot to process for them. I feel better, at least, being able to them we've got a bad guy."

They both leaned back in their chairs and took a breath and calculated where they stood like at the turn of the flop. Logan rested his eyes.

"So here's what we're going to do," said Days. "Don't go anywhere for a while. We might need to call you in and talk some more. We might still lay charges. We'll probably be calling you as a witness."

Logan looked down at his shoes while he thought about things.

"And we need that car as evidence."

"That's between you and Ricky," said Logan. "It's his car. You'll need a warrant."

Detective Days tongued on something stuck in his teeth and closed his eyes and shook his head. He leaned forward again and squinted at Logan.

"You are on my last nerve," said Days. "Get out of here."

Logan stood around Champion City Pawn flipping through old DVDs while he waited for Ricky to show up. Ricky exploded through the front door with a cigarette in his mouth.

"We can smoke in here now?" asked the dopey-eyed pawn broker at the counter.

"Absolutely the fuck not," said Ricky, plucking the cigarette out of his mouth and blowing out his nose in twin columns. "Only I may smoke in here."

Clare followed him in through the front door with a big backpack on her back. She walked in close to Logan by the DVD rack.

"Thanks, big brother," she said.

Logan nodded.

"That your book bag?"

"We bought all my books today," she said.

"Nerd."

She gave him a shot in the arm and he pushed her back.

Ricky snapped his fingers.

"Logan, come on."

Logan winked at Clare and followed Ricky into the back and down the stairs to the basement. They squeezed through the hallway cluttered with bikes all the way to his office and when they got there Ricky pulled the string connected to the single bare light bulb on the ceiling.

Ricky ran a finger along the edge of his desk as he slinked around it to his seat. Logan slumped down in one of the ripped and faded office chairs facing it.

"Good job getting the car," said Ricky and he let that hang in the air. He cocked his head back and looked over his cheek bones at Logan. "There's some heat around it, isn't there?"

Whatever expression was on Logan's face caused Ricky to change his tack.

"Best I don't know, I guess," he said. "First things first, I need to get that phone back off you. Pissy Chrissie has been coming around here asking for it. I didn't think she'd come back for it in a million years but here she is. I've been saying it's in my 'other' safe."

Logan dug the phone out of his pocket and put it on Ricky's desk.

"You look shell shocked. You OK?"

"I'm fine," said Logan.

Ricky opened his file drawer and pulled out a contract.

"This is the loan agreement for the money I gave you," he said. He pulled out a rubber stamp and stamped 'Paid In Full' across Logan's signature.

"You guys bought her books today, hey?"

Ricky chuckled.

"You should see some of the kids running around that school," he said. "Your sister has got a few years on them but that life experience will probably help her out, I think. Does it seem like college students are younger than they used to be?"

"I think we just get older," said Logan.

"You might be right. Some of them looked barely out of diapers."

Ricky slid the stamped piece of paper to one side.

"So how are you doing for money?" Ricky asked.

Logan shrugged.

"You need something to get you by?"

Logan shrugged again.

Ricky pulled out a blank loan agreement.

"What do you think, two grand enough to get you by?"

Logan didn't move.

Ricky opened a drawer and pulled out a fresh contract and a pen. He copied over the information from the previous loan agreement to the new one.

"You don't know anywhere to sell animal skins, do you?" he asked without looking up as he transcribed the information on the contracts.

"I don't," said Logan.

"I got my peepee whacked for trying to sell some online. I guess you're not supposed to."

Ricky finished writing and signed off at the bottom with a flourish. He slid the papers over to Logan and smacked the pen down on top. He lifted a locked metal box out from a drawer in the desk. From there, he pulled out a wad of bills. While Logan initialed and signed the contract in all the usual places, Ricky counted out fifty and hundred dollar bills in tidy stacks at the edge of the table in front of Logan.

Logan swept them up and stuffed them into his wallet.

"Don't spend it all in one place," Ricky said with a wry smile.

The doors had been repaired since Logan was last at Klondike Casino and he was greeted with tall, shiny glass doors that smelled of Windex.

"Has it been two weeks already?" said Gus, the head of security, when he looked up and saw Logan walk in the front door. He stood up from his perch behind the entryway greeting counter.

Logan nodded at him with an uptick of his head.

"Well, you know the rules. We have to talk to the pit boss first."

Gus led them along a shortcut between the VLT machines.

"How you been, Logan?" asked Gus as they walked between rows of machines flashing reds and yellows and gold.

"Good. You?"

"Still alive."

Gus led them over to the bar where a guy who looked like a failed Vegas lounge singer leaned against the edge, going over a work schedule. He had bouffant dark hair with white stripes on the sides and thick eyebrows like big black fuzzy caterpillars.

The pit boss looked up at Logan, the caterpillars on his forehead arching their backs, and then looked back down at the staffing schedule and said, "Logan."

"Sorry for last time," said Logan. "I was going through some stuff and had a bad day but that's over with now."

"We're trying to run a nice establishment here," said the pit boss. "We're trying to attract a certain kind of clientele. We can't have people screaming and fighting like maniacs. That's bush league. That's not us."

"I understand," said Logan.

"You going to be good?"

"Yeah."

"Can I buy you a beer?" asked the pit boss.

"Sure."

"Ashley, a Gold Star for my friend here," said the pit boss.

The young woman behind the bar knelt down to the beer fridge and swiveled back up with a Gold Star in her hand and plunked it down in front of Logan.

"Thank you," said Logan.

"Alright," said the pit boss. "Go have some fun."

Gus stayed behind to chat with the pit boss and the bartender as Logan walked to the window. The woman with the big 1980s hair and sparkling blue eyeshadow at the window did a weak job of holding back a knowing smile as she took his money and handed him a tray of chips. Then he settled himself down at a Hold 'Em table.

The other players were a strange mixture of every other player he had ever faced. Unshaven. Dark rings under their eyes. Ball caps. Sunglasses.

The blinds slid clockwise from one player to the next. The dealer slung cards to the other players around the table. Logan pressed one palm down on his cards and lifted the corners to give his cards a peek. A King-Queen, suited diamonds. Twenty-four percent chance of winning against six other players pre-flop. He slid a couple chips in front of him.

He looked around. The VLTs chimed. The servers strutted around calling out the names of cocktails. The boys at the bar slipped booze into their pints of Coke and stared up at the football replays.

"Sir?" asked the dealer.

Logan turned around to face the table.

"Check, raise, fold?"

Logan lifted the corners again to give his cards another peek and then tapped the backs twice with his fingers.

Thanks for reading. If you liked it, please leave a review. If you didn't like it, then don't. Just kidding. I don't care what you do.

Follow the author on Twitter: @edmontonnoir

Follow the author on Instagram: @edmontonnoir

Email the author: edmontonnoir@protonmail.com

About the Author

Kenneth Price is a thief, a scoundrel, and a lowdown, dirty, rotten snake. His days are filled with alcohol and destruction. Behind him lies a trail of broken hearts of all the people who tried to care for him but he lashed out from self-loathing. He lives in Edmonton.

Lightning Source UK Ltd.
Milton Keynes UK
UKHW010650150622
404464UK00002B/393